LIVING LEGENDARY

A NOVEL

To: Nick and Nicole

LIVING LEGENDARY

A NOVEL

JON PEARLMAN

Enjoy the book and
Keep Living Legendary!

Jon Pearlman
5/27/17

PUBLISHING HOUSE

An Evolve Publishing House Book
This edition first published 2016, by Evolve Publishing House, LLC,
Florida, United States of America.

Library of Congress Cataloging-in-Publication Data
Library of Congress Control Number: 2016912768
Name: Pearlman, Jon, 1988— author.
Title: Living Legendary : A Novel / Jon Pearlman.
Description: Florida : Evolve Publishing House, LLC, [2016]
Identifiers: ISBN 978-0-9907859-0-3 (paperback)
Subjects: LCSH : American Satire (sh85117648)
                Humorous Stories (sh85062975)
                Physical Fitness—United States (sh2010106291)
                Physical Fitness—Nutritional Aspects (sh85101541)
                Self-help techniques (sh85119759)
Classification: DDC : 813/.6
228 p. 20 cm.

ONE

Cardboardmag.com/Living_Legendary_Blog

While everyone's been debating whether gravity is on its way out (#theendofgravity?), there's been some other very interesting activity in certain corners of the Internet: the "Living Legendary" blog (livinglegendaryblog.com, @lvnglgndry). At the helm of this head-scratching site is Jon Brody — a former Ivy League athlete — who has managed to secure over 500k page views last month alone. But with posts like, "Orgasm from Organics," "The Legendary Erection," and "Work Out Naked," people have started to ask: "Is this real — or some type of spoof?"

We met with the Living Legendary founder at the Cardboard Mag offices earlier this week to get some answers.

Cardboard Mag: We would like to start off by asking you the obvious question that's been on all of our minds: Is your blog real, or is this all one big joke?

Jon Brody: I'm sorry — was that question real? Please don't insult me.

CM: Your lifestyle seems a bit extreme. Do you think "normal" people can and should adhere to your advice?

Jon Brody: Living Legends are inherently *not* normal. They stand apart and are elevated from the masses. If you're a normal person and you're seeking a lifestyle framework, Living Legendary isn't the one for you. It's exclusively for those who want to separate from the crowd. For those who want to become something great.

CM: Your audience has been growing at an impressive rate. To what do you attribute this?

Jon Brody: Legendary content. People will naturally gravitate towards quality material. And my number one priority is churning out top-notch posts. The majority of social media personalities invest in the wrong channels: tweeting forty times per day, or paying off Instagram for more followers. There's nothing Legendary about 140 characters or false hype. Living Legends produce 140 *pages*.

CM: Your "about page" says you've written a book. Why hasn't this been released yet?

Jon Brody: Oh, it's coming. Trust me.

CM: If there's one piece of advice for your fans to follow, assuming they can't do it all, what would it be?

Jon Brody: Well, first and foremost, people should know that you can't cherry-pick bits of my program and become a Living Legend. That will never work. Legends adhere to all of the necessary principles. Every one of them.

CM: Final question: You advocate for the "Legendary erection" and discuss how to go about having "amazing sex." What would be your number one bit of advice for someone looking to maximize his or her sex life.

Jon Brody: Be open-minded. Especially with respect to unconventional mechanisms for intimacy. Legends never shut any doors.

LivingLegendaryBlog.com/About

Living Legendary is a unique approach to life that helps people combine physical and mental capacities to reach their full potential.

The first step is perfecting your nutrition and fitness regimens, because you can only become a Living Legend if you achieve peak physical form. The Living Legendary Framework details how you can convert your midnight snack into a midnight workout, and turn that six-pack of Budweiser into six-pack abs.

The second component is achieving a sound mental approach to your life at large. This entails seeing the world from a Legendary perspective — and fine-tuning your behavior accordingly. Living Legends go about their lives with a clear head and a critical eye.

The final step to Living Legendary is doing just that: Living Legendary. You will be able to pinpoint the most attractive girl in the room and acquire her number (sober), jump from a five-story window unscathed, burn off the calories from three meals in 30 minutes, write a 200-

page book in the course of a day, and perpetually go about life with sky-high confidence and a "can-do-anything" attitude, as if you just snorted a line. Once you're a Living Legend you will know it because the indicators are too hard to miss.

It's time to start moving yourself in the right direction and finally take back control of your life. It's time to start Living Legendary.

Meet Jon Brody

Jon Brody has been Living Legendary ever since he couldn't find a date to the high school prom. From that point onwards, Jon — or, "The Legend" — dedicated himself to becoming a better man and a model citizen, one who would never be without a beautiful woman on his arm.

For the past decade, The Legend has pursued a lifestyle grounded in physical, mental, and spiritual growth. A decorated athlete and graduate of the Ivy League, Jon Brody knows what it takes to arrive at Legendary status — and, since graduating from college one year ago, has dedicated himself to helping others reach their full potential. In his short career, Brody has already proven he should be regarded as one of the leaders of the new-age diet and fitness industry. He helped a morbidly obese high-schooler shed 150 pounds by handcuffing him to a cooler of raw vegetables. He worked diligently with a group of pyromaniacs to burn down three fast food restaurants (casualty-free). He spent a week camped out in his neighborhood supermarket with a taser, shocking patrons who reached for non-organic produce. You don't become a Living Legend for nothing, something Jon Brody understands better than anyone — and he's here to assist you in moving swiftly along the right path.

Brody's new book, "The Living Legendary Framework," is set for release at the end of this year — and once his way of life catches on, the world will never be the same. In the meantime, follow the Living Legendary Blog and begin to invest in your Legend.

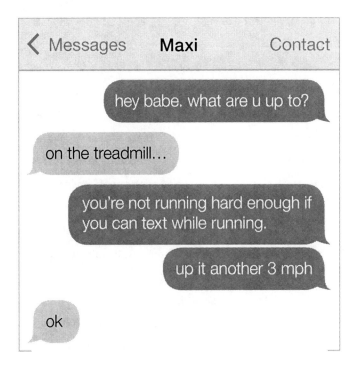

LivingLegendaryBlog.com

Analyze Your Food Habits

It's important that you think critically about your food habits
in order to gauge whether or not they are up to Living Legendary
standards. If you find yourself frequenting a buffet, with the cuisine of
origin ending in the letters "-ese" — Chinese, Japanese, Portuguese
(a.k.a. Brazilian steakhouse) — or if you (or your company) have found
entertainment in the fact that your restaurant's chairs *are on wheels*
(even worse if it's in an Olive Garden), your food trajectory isn't what
it ought to be. If you're at a sandwich counter (problematic to begin
with) and you're ordering a sub with "extra mayo," offering a muffled
explanation ("I really like mayo") — or if you're salivating all day at
the office flipping through "food porn" memes, there's a unique (well,
maybe not so unique) problem to be addressed. If you find yourself
inside a McDonald's (or, worse, if your family is there with you), eyes
closed and thanking God for the "food" in front of you — or if you ever
smoke, chew gum, dip, drink diet soda, or pop caffeine pills to control

your caloric intake, you're not on the path towards Legendary.

Suppose you drink a six-pack of beer or a whole bottle of wine *each night*, or you experience sadness when you're on the last bite of your "Five Guys" burger (because that's your daily "high" and it's about to end). Or maybe you're eating breakfast in bed, or you're trying to figure out what the hell that person at the checkout aisle will be doing with a pint of *fresh* blueberries. Or forget the sight of blueberries, because you're crammed together with fifteen other girls for "movie night," eating a spread of brownies, pies, cakes, cookies, ice-cream, cream puffs, whipped cream, and creamsicles — and posting a picture on social media with the (alarmingly proud) caption, "Girls Do Movie Night." If you adhere to the "Jack in the Box" slogan, "Hunger has no curfew" — your Living Legendary status isn't where it needs to be.

COMMENTS (1)

STUPID

Jon Brody you're pathetic. Graduate from the Ivy League and this sham of a site is all you can come up with. What a waste. 500k page views per month? You must spend an awful lot of time hitting refresh, loser.

< Messages   **Ma**   Contact

Just ran into Cathy Benedict on the street and she asked about you. Said you were still living at home.

Ok

Patrick is working at Morgan and living in the city.

What does that have to do with me?

I told her you're a writer.

I'm an innovator more than a writer.

Sweetie. How did this happen to us? 😕😟

From: Jon Brody
To: Scott Samson
Subject: Query

Dear Mr. Samson,

I'm writing because I'm an Ivy League grad with a proposal and manuscript I hope I might be able to interest you in taking a look at. I've written a book for ambitious millennials, a self-help book titled THE LIVING LEGENDARY FRAMEWORK.

I graduated from the Ivy League last spring, and as a student-athlete I experienced shock seeing how poorly so many of my teammates — and classmates — treated their bodies and treated their minds. One teammate would arrive at afternoon practices still drunk from the previous night, but would push himself through with periodic intravenous injections of liquid Adderall. One sociology student who sat next to me during lecture would regularly down two full-size pizzas and three liters of Coke, a strange routine given I often noticed him eating several plates at lunch in the cafeteria beforehand. A teaching assistant for an economics section was obese to the point he couldn't stand and — refusing to operate the white board from his wheelchair — would select four or five shrinking students in the front row to prop him up each time he sought the felt pen (several of these students acquired hernias in the process).

My book is a starting point for young people hoping to follow a path similar to mine — a path free of drinking, drugs, overeating, and obesity-induced wheelchairs — and I hope the first in a series of books building a full lifestyle brand. I have a completed manuscript that I can send you, and I've launched a website with regular blog updates. I'm hoping this might be something that will appeal and I'd love to work together if so.

Best,

Jon Brody

> **fitbiatch** Everyone knows the biggest meal of the day should be breakfast, not dinner!
>
> **lvnglgndry** That was just a Kelloggs marketing ploy to get you to buy more cereal. The order should be: (1) big dinner, (2) light breakfast, (3) massive workout.
>
> **fitbiatch** I think you don't know what the hell you're talking about. Btw just went to your site. R u some kind of cult leader?

The Living Legendary Framework, Book Proposal Introduction

30% of college students today — an all-time high — are overweight or obese. At the same time, on the academic side the United States is falling behind the rest of the world. We're in a downward spiral — and no one out there is speaking to young people, in a voice they will listen to, about how to find success across the spectrum: succeeding academically, athletically, and living fit, healthy, happy lives. With LIVING LEGENDARY, I am set to change that — to be the leader of a new generation of ambitious youth ready to live successful, optimized lives trampling upon the ruins of their obese, impotent, intellectually-bankrupt peers. As a decorated student-athlete of the Ivy League just a year out of school, I have lived the life that thousands of young people aspire to — or at least ought to — and I have emerged with a fully-developed framework for maximizing life, applicable not just to the beer-gut-plagued frat bro, but to anyone who wishes to follow the path to health, happiness, and success.

This is not just another convenient gift option for the awkward high-schooler or sexually-stunted college freshman — it's the first entry in a new category of literature for young people, offering a complete life transformation to anyone able and willing to listen. With a growing social media presence, a developed marketing plan, a television pilot in the making, and a fully-written manuscript ready to go, LIVING LEGENDARY is set to be the next big movement among men and women ages 16-24.

Not just an advice book but an introduction to an entirely new way to live, LIVING LEGENDARY tackles nutrition, exercise, health and productivity through a revolutionary new framework developed by the author during his time in the Ivy League. The book presents a three-step plan:

1.) Why You're Obese and How to Correct It

2.) Adopting a Sound Mental Approach

3.) Start Living Legendary

Within those categories, LIVING LEGENDARY provides unexpected wisdom, designed to make self-help cool, young, and current. Why you should become a "nightlife shark" — seeking out potential romantic partners at their peak levels of intoxication, while you stay sober. How to stay athletic into adulthood, joining afterschool sports leagues and summer camps without the threat of charges that you're a sexual predator. Why you should convince your girlfriend she's overweight and prescribe a fitness program so intense it curtails any chance of her continuing to menstruate.

The term "Living Legendary" has never before been used in

this way — and the hashtag "#livinglegendary" has already caught on with many social media followers. Moreover, the stories shared in the book's pages are unique, captivating, and bring the Living Legendary plan to life.

The website platform for the book — LivingLegendaryBlog.com — has been launched and is already building an audience with regular blog posts and video updates. The television pilot, a make-over reality program modeled after *The Biggest Loser* in which Jon Brody assists seemingly "healthy weight" people in their attempts to lose upwards of 30 pounds, is entering the final stages of test subject recruitment.

There is a population eager and hungry for this book (although once Brody's through with them, they won't be experiencing much hunger at all) — from Ivy League-aspirants all the way down the line, looking to change their lives for the better, overtake their peers, and finally start Living Legendary.

From: Michael Brody
To: Jon Brody
Subject: Book

Jon,

Great seeing you the other day. I know you're busy, or at least you say you are. Maybe you can try to make time a little more often. Would be good to see you more regularly. Your book project sounds interesting, I suppose, although I'm not sure I see it the same way you do. My first take is that an Ivy League degree won't be enough to put you in the position of a life-advice personality. You will probably need some work experience first to establish yourself.

Your dad

From: Jon Brody
To: Michael Brody
Subject: RE: Book

Thanks for the input, but the book is much more than an Ivy degree talking. It's from years of pursuing my athletic lifestyle, which, had you supported more, you probably would have a better idea of. I want to hold off on any more get-togethers until I've made more progress with the agent search. I did mail a copy of the manuscript to the apartment though, so you should have it sometime this week.

P.S. Are you planning on taking more luxury vacations this year — or was the two-month-long European excursion sufficient? By the way does Barry even know where you got all that money?

From: Michael Brody
To: Jon Brody
Subject: RE: RE: Book

Tried calling you but no answer. The topics you're bringing up aren't appropriate for email. I was behind you pursuing sports but not in the way you and Ma went about it. In my opinion, you didn't need to relocate four states away for training. That was excessive and I wasn't going to fund it. Also, don't appreciate the vacation remark. I'll take another trip when I want, and for however long I want to. It's my money and I'll be bringing Barry with me.

From: Jon Brody
To: Michael Brody
Subject: RE: RE: RE: Book

YOUR money?! What a joke. The truth will get out sooner or later.
Dad turning gay just wasn't enough, was it…
P.S. Without that training, I never would have made it to the Ivy
League. It's the sports that got me in, not your Tennessee Tech legacy.

From: Michael Brody
To: Jon Brody
Subject: RE: RE: RE: RE: Book

Just remember: you're only as good as your last project. You've been
out of school eight months now. The Ivy League isn't in the rear-view
mirror anymore…

TWO

The Living Legendary Framework, Manuscript
Chapter 1: There's No Paradox. You're Obese.

<u>Introduction</u>

I'll tell it to your face because no one else will: you're obese. (You probably suspected. I'm now verifying it.) I'm not doing it to make you feel bad, or to elevate myself in some way. I'm saying what needs to be said, and it's in your best interest to hear it.

The truth is never easy, but correcting your problems necessarily has to involve seeing them for what they are. That's where I step in. To set you straight. To get you back on course. To skyrocket you out of your decades-long denial, your undeserved comfort, your wanting-to-do-something-but-never-have roadblock — so you can finally start Living Legendary.

Forget the Fat Acceptance Movement and the notion that "heavier is healthier." It's not. "Heavier" is shameful. It's disgusting. It's horrifying. It's reason enough to be put down.

You want to be fit. You want to look good. You want to feel sexy. Accept these things and start making a change. Hell, it's not just about looking good. It's about responsibility. To yourself. To your wife. To your kids. To the little boy next to you on the airplane, flying without a guardian and steadily disappearing beneath your love handle.

Being fat isn't an illness and it isn't genetically acquired — and it's certainly not some paradox. Nor is it something to feel good about or accept. If you're obese, there's a reason you're obese. Now correct it. The first step to doing so — in 99 percent of cases — is revamping your nutrition. You probably aren't fat if you aren't eating poorly.

I know bad eating habits because I lived them. In fact, I come from a family of obesity. My mother had unique advice for maintaining a healthy corporal equilibrium: "If you're already hungry, it's too late." It resulted in a childhood of overeating. I remember one time when she made me eat half a dozen Krispy Kreme donuts after dinner when I didn't finish my plate of meat loaf because she wanted me to know what it really felt like to be full, and understand that feeling any less stuffed meant I didn't get enough nutrition.

It took many years before I realized I was heading down a deleterious path. And it took even more time to change course. You may not have that much time. That's why I'm here.

The Living Legendary Framework, as I'm sure you've gathered by now, won't coddle you and tell you everything's okay. It's straight talk for those who want to improve. It's real talk for those who aren't afraid to open their eyes and start asking the right questions. It's candid perspective to ignite the fire within and spur you to action. It's a catalyst that may very well save your life in the process.

The Living Legendary Framework isn't just about shedding the excess weight, as you'll learn in the pages to come. It's about making the right choices — with respect to food *and life*. Living Legends aren't born. They're made. Through willpower, commitment, and resolve — displayed day-in and day-out for a decades-long period. But we have to start somewhere, and there's no better place than your eating habits.

A Passion for Obesity

I know obesity first-hand and it isn't pretty. My family's obese. My friends are obese. My girlfriend is obese. Even my dog is obese.

Drowning in this sea of obesity has certainly taken a toll on my psyche, but in my particular case, the mental damage has transformed into passion. I have a passion for obesity.

My passion for obesity has prompted me to craft a nutritional approach that will facilitate real, lasting results. Some might say my routines are unmanageable, my viewpoints extreme.   But I will be upfront in saying that there is no smooth-sailing ride to the six-pack promised land.

Some years ago, my Uncle Larry — well over 350 pounds for decades — miraculously shed his excess weight within a few short months. When I saw Uncle Larry post-regimen, he was rail-thin to the point of being unrecognizable. The problem with his program, however, was that he died within several weeks of reaching featherweight status.

Upon his passing, it was soon discovered that he had patented the smoothie recipe that facilitated his 200-pound, two-month program. Larry's son, Larry Jr., a gambling addict who was in deep with the Russian mafia, frantically discussed the possibility with other immediate family members of marketing and selling Larry's miracle weight loss drink.

While the smoothie never did make it to shelves, and Larry Jr. never did make it to his next poker game (his body was found some days later in the North Fork river, the family benefiting from significant savings at the funeral home on account of a joint service), the episode of the Larry's played an instrumental role in developing the Living Legendary approach, for I witnessed the extreme version of what can happen when you follow an off-base nutritional strategy. My advice is based on many years of experience in transforming my own body, and in assisting those who were able and willing to listen (primarily residents of the local retirement home). If nothing else, you can trust me given the fact I'm still alive (or at least I was at the point this went to press).

So snap on your seatbelt — or, if you're one of the severe cases, snap together all three extensions — because we're heading off on a memorable ride... one that doesn't involve pit-stopping for a "Super Big Gulp."

Let's do this. Let's start tackling obesity head on.

From: Michael Brody
To: Jon Brody
Subject: "The Larry's"

Jon,

I received the copy of the manuscript and started reading. You're going to have to take out the "Larry's Story" (a.k.a. Uncle Harry and Cousin

Harry). This information can't go outside of the family.
I will write once I've gotten through more. I'm proud of you.
Your Dad.

LivingLegendaryBlog.com

Rolling Chairs

I would like to briefly expand on the issue of rolling chairs raised in an earlier post, and why it's problematic to frequent restaurants that feature them — specifically the Olive Garden. The Olive Garden has put much thought into the layout, décor, dish selection, and ambience of its restaurants, and the fact that its chairs are on wheels is not by chance. Corporate management knows its patrons are largely obese. Post-meal, these oversized people might well have difficulty maneuvering themselves out of an ordinary legged chair. "A rolling chair will slide back effortlessly," the CEO might have said one day, "removing the possibility of any physical or mental discomfort. Not to mention allowing their protruding stomachs to elevate without knocking over the table in the process, certainly saving us money from having to replace broken dishes and glasses, or the cost of employing extra busboys. Rolling chairs it is. End of meeting."

From: Scott Samson
To: Jon Brody
Subject: Re: Query

Dear Jon: Is this a prank of some kind? I really don't appreciate you
querying me with this type of material. I'm overweight, and I don't
doubt you've seen photos of me given they're all over the web. I do
like Sonic and I plan to keep eating there. And I think most readers out
there are a lot more like me than you. At least google people before you
query them and make sure you're not personally insulting them. Also,
just because you're fat doesn't make you "disgusting," "pathetic," or a
"social burden" — although it's certainly impressive you were able to
include all three of these descriptions in the first two paragraphs (after
which point I stopped reading, by the way).

I would recommend you put some time into rethinking what you're
saying before you query other agents. All of us have similar minds
(and lifestyles). If you were smart you'd realize that most people who
read voraciously don't work out. If they did, they wouldn't be reading
voraciously. It's a circular feedback loop of sorts. Anyway, I don't have
more time here — I've got a box of chicken tenders and a milkshake to
finish. And some reading to do too.   Scott Samson

TWEETS	FOLLOWING	FOLLOWERS	FAVORITES	LISTS
400	5K	80K	1,000	3

Tweets   Tweets & replies   Photos & videos

Living Legendary @LvngLgndry · 10h
You're better off dying thin than living fat
#livinglegendary #eatbokchoy #lean

↩ 0   ♻ 1   ★ 0

The Living Legendary Framework, Manuscript Chapter 10: Origins of Living Legendary. The Shaping of the Framework

<u>Never Compromise on Your Health and Passion</u>

It was the spring of my sophomore year and I was twenty years old. I had just come off an incredibly successful season where I had become the star player of the team. My background in sports as a high-schooler was mediocre at best, and I could not have imagined coming this far. I was finally gaining real confidence in my abilities, and it seemed as though the hard work and sweat I had put into athletics was leading to a worthwhile destination.

Yet at some point during that spring semester, the reality settled in that I'd better start preparing another course for myself. Whether it was the fact that my best friend at the time had just been hired by Goldman Sachs, or the discussions about my future that I was having with my parents, I started to think about the "bigger picture." Sure, the athletic success I was enjoying was great, but the reality was that I wasn't going to be a professional sportsman and so I had better start sowing the seeds for my future, or so I thought.

With these new concerns taking hold, I took the necessary steps (with the help of parental connections) to line up an internship for the summer. I understood my time for sports training would be limited, but I figured that a concerted effort to stay in shape should do the job in keeping me fit for my junior-year season. I had been able to balance school and athletics thus far, and I was certain I could do the same during the internship. After all, I couldn't continue a sports-focused lifestyle forever, right? It was going to end at some point soon, so I had better start moving my life in a more practical direction.

Flash forward: the internship is now underway. I am commuting daily from central Manhattan to Tenafly, New Jersey, where I am working for a real estate private equity fund. While I was a bit unsure about what I was getting into at the outset, one day at the office made it crystal clear: a daily schedule of two hours in the car, ten at the desk, and thirty minutes of exercise in the morning if I was lucky not to sleep past the five o'clock alarm — with negligible (if any) actual output, since the internship was merely being used as a resume-builder and the firm didn't have any substantial work for me.

Sitting at the desk that first day for eleven hours (my friend at Goldman recommended I stay extra late to make a good impression), staring at a blank Windows desktop screen (given my sparse workload, I had no need to turn it on), I wondered how I was going to explain to my family and the head of the firm (who did my family a huge favor in getting me the job) that I did not think this was the life for me. As I drove back into Manhattan over the George Washington Bridge that evening, with bumper-to-bumper traffic on the other side of the road, I contemplated for a brief moment ending my life right there by making a sudden, sharp turn.

The days pass and I'm jumping out of my skin, but I keep face and stick to the routine. I ease the boredom of the cubicle by independently assigning myself to the firm's "blue collar" duties — stocking the copiers with paper, picking up lunch orders, filling the coffee machine, setting the rat-poison traps, and sweeping the carpets. My boss, observing my daily rounds and worrying that one of my family members might see this on a surprise visit, decides to get me out of the office by sending me to one of the firm's local properties — a subsidized housing project. I'm instructed to obtain signatures from the tenants, which will authorize government-backed renovations the firm will avoid having to pay for on account of a recently-passed energy-efficiency bill. As I trek from apartment to apartment in Black Label Ralph Lauren in the midday heat, knocking on doors (the bulk of which aren't answered), a matte black, souped-up Dodge Challenger with tinted windows, engine running and vibrating from the heavy bass being played inside, is permanently stationed in one of the two handicapped parking spaces closest to the complex. On visiting the premises later with colleagues, it is brought to my attention that a massive drug operation is being run out of #403C — but the firm hadn't been successful yet in evicting the tenant. Forget about exercise — the bulk of my energies are now allocated to monitoring the Challenger from the corner of my eye, perpetually on the ready to duck at a moment's notice should automatic weapons open fire.

With my physical training regimen at a standstill, I begin to decondition — and rapidly. When I get back from a multi-hour stretch at the housing project, I look at myself in the firm's bathroom mirror (the only time I have away from the "fish bowl" office setup) and observe visible signs of atrophy — and I know my sports game is going along with it. After a few weeks, I cave completely, neglecting my early morning workouts. I meet friends out at bars several nights each week and on the weekends, staying out late and accruing a sleep deficit. I hardly drank before this point, yet I soon find myself throwing back three or four cocktails each night. Without any time to prepare my own food, I begin eating all of my meals out of the house — and the weight piles on. Before I even realize it, I'm following a lifestyle completely contrary to everything known to me beforehand.

A month and a half in, my thoughts begin to circulate. Why did I throw away my athletic progress for this? Is this office life my final destination — the one I've been working so hard for all these years? Why haven't these office people killed themselves by now? It's been only a few weeks and I'm already close.

Relevant here is my high school upbringing — namely the cutthroat competitive environment of the New York City private school system, where students wrestle with each other to the death for a few spots in the Ivy League. In the beginning, I simply fought to stay afloat. But soon, as my skill set expanded and my resilience mounted, I grew tenacious like the rest and wanted a share of the pie. My whole childhood was spent head down and working — studying like the professional I was supposed to be. Any time outside of studying was used for athletic training, and so the concept of recreation — a weekend night with friends, perhaps — simply didn't exist. The hard work paid off when I was offered Ivy League admission — yet even then it didn't seem like there was a minute for celebration. There was a new concern: how to out-do my Ivy League counterparts for a better summer job, for a higher-paying career path.

Back to Tenafly. The pride of the office is the forty-five-year-old data manager: a bald, full-stomached, sickly-looking gentleman who, due to his relentless drive and passion for Excel spreadsheets, hadn't taken a day of vacation in six years. Whether or not he was financially compensated for such over-the-top dedication to the company (I'm wagering not) still remained a mystery, yet he stood strong as a model for what we all should aspire towards. Dark eye circles, pale complexion, muscle-less limbs, chronic back pain — no matter; the "data wizard" was moving up in the world, at least if you asked his superiors.

With the wizard front and center, foreshadowing my future self, I soon came to the conclusion that life no longer had much to offer me. Any lingering trace of a positive outlook disintegrated. My mind began to wander. I couldn't engage in conversations without drifting off. I started to feel tremendous anxiety about completing even simple tasks. I would wake up each morning with racing thoughts, and couldn't shut them off. I was unable to read a few paragraphs and understand their meaning.

Upon arriving on campus that fall, I couldn't navigate my way to classes. If I did manage to make it to the lecture hall, my mind would be elsewhere while the professor spoke. I tried to create a schedule with the easiest possible classes, hoping I could find my bearings, but even those seemed far beyond what I could manage. I was soon forced to withdraw from school.

Arriving home — my family in panic — I was immediately sent to a slew of doctors who diagnosed me with various psychological afflictions. I had lost control over my mind, my functionality as a human completely and utterly incapacitated. From a star athlete with a 4.0 GPA, I had been rendered a mental cripple, unable to read a sentence or engage in basic discussion. I was anxious and unable to focus. And it wasn't just my mind that was finished — my body was too. I couldn't sleep. I had no appetite or sex drive. Since the beginning of the summer, I had gained nearly thirty pounds.

It took me a full year to recover, although it required many more to overcome the psychological damage. I was able to use sports and exercise to divert my attention from the crisis at hand — and help me heal. Time passed and I once again began to foster some mental clarity. After a year away, I re-entered the Ivy League... but as a completely different person: fearful, uncertain, and reserved. I took each day as a separate challenge — working to get ahead on my studies, focusing on my sports practices, and occupying my mind at all times so my thoughts would keep still (especially at night, before I fell asleep). Fearful that at any point my mind could collapse, I worked to finish assignments months in advance. In one class, I handed in the final term paper five weeks ahead of time — something the professor, in thirty years of teaching, had never seen before. Harnessing my discipline and drive, I pushed through my doubts and fears and made it through the first year back. It was this initial hump that proved the hardest, because from then on I started to understand more clearly what was necessary to secure my mental and physical health.

This story ties directly into what it means to Live Legendary because it illustrates what can happen when a person succumbs to outside influence and societal pressure — and is steered onto a course at odds with his or her passions. It's usually the case that an individual pushed in a harmful direction doesn't realize it at first, or even suspect that anything is wrong until the damage has accrued and it's almost too severe to reverse. In my own case, the time period of the decline was relatively short, yet the damage increased exponentially with each passing day. More than anything, my story is a warning for acquiescence, for accepting a path contrary to what's right for you, and moving along on an "accepted" route of prestige or validation when that route is harmful to your health and well being.

Living Legendary is a lifestyle that prioritizes staying true to yourself. It is one that puts mental and physical health above all else. Living Legendary means analyzing the everyday to understand whether your routine jibes with who you are and what you want to become. It means understanding that accepting a set of circumstances contrary to your best interests can (and likely, will) lead to profound negative effects and sometimes irreparable damage. The path to Legendary isn't easy, but once you start finding your footing and committing to your direction, you will soon realize that you aren't far off.

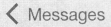

< Messages   **Ma**   Contact

Did you move the cake mix? The Greens are coming later and I'm going to bake.

The only thing you should be baking are sweet potatoes. I threw it out.

Btw I also threw out the Munchies Snack Mix, chocolate chips, ice cream sandwiches, and fudgesicles.

And everything in the pantry.

What?! You have no right doing that. This is MY HOUSE!

I'm helping you Ma

You will pay to replace all of this. Start figuring out how.

LivingLegendaryBlog.com

Get Lean

Living Legendary means pursuing the lean body — but "getting lean" doesn't just pertain to the physical because you need to shed weight across the board. This means eliminating excess baggage in life: unnecessary possessions, superficial friends, and extended family members. Get rid of the extra ten pairs of jeans in your closet, and sever ties with the loser you met at the bar last weekend. Time to forget about your second cousin Alberto along with your Godson Luke (what the hell is a "Godson" anyway and who needs one?).

Let's start focusing on what's important: becoming Legendary. There's no more time for formalities or the false belief that extended ties (or a second pair of sunglasses) will get you somewhere. You have limited time and energy, and these precious resources should be invested with efficiency.

COMMENTS (1)

OFFENSIVE

I grew up without my biological father and it was my godfather who raised me. What you're saying isn't nice. Stop it.

From: Jon Brody
To: Magnus Johansen
Subject: Mentor

Dear Mr. Johansen,

I was the author who called into the Siriux XM studio today at 1:23pm and asked you the question: "If you had one piece of advice for the creative artist looking to break through, what would it be?" Your response — "Believe in what you're doing. And never give up" — has been incredibly inspirational, and I wanted to thank you for your advice. I aspire to someday rise to the top of the publishing ranks in the same way you have in the EDM world. If by any chance you would like to serve as my mentor in this process, please let me know. I would be delighted to have you on board the Living Legendary team.

I hope to hear from you and again I want you to know I am a big fan.

Best, Jon Brody

‹ Messages   Maxi   Contact

If we ever have a baby I want him lean.

lol

I'm not kidding.

LivingLegendaryBlog.com

A Few Useful Questions

(1) How do you know if you're actually hungry and not just experiencing food cravings? Simple. If you aren't finding cold oatmeal, steamed chard, raw whole radishes, or canned sardines appetizing, then your hunger is short of where it needs to be.

(2) How do you know if what you ate was Legendary-grade? First, you should pay close attention to the effort involved in chewing. Difficulty of mastication is always proportional to nutritional quality. Each forkful should require at least 2-3 minutes of mouth-work. This is one major reason Living Legends never socialize during

meals (we will address the others to come). The same holds true for food shopping and preparation. The heavier it is to carry and the harder it is to prepare (washing, cutting, cooking), the better. Last, make note of your burping post-meal. If the air is flowing up freely without accompanying food chunks, the food was high-quality. If you're having difficulty purging your chest gas, the contents were subpar.

(3) Why do you only see fat people eating food labeled as "skinny" — "Skinny Cow" ice cream sandwiches, "Skinny Pop" Popcorn, and "Skinnygirl" nutrition bars? Ice cream, popcorn, and (cleverly-marketed) candy bars make you fat.

(4) Why are you filling out a quiz on Facebook to determine "what kind of food you are?" Send a full body shot of yourself (Instagram filter-free) to the Living Legendary Headquarters and Jon Brody will identify your food type. Based on recent submissions, the majority are fried chicken or pizza.

COMMENTS (2)

DORSEY

I eat Skinny Pop Popcorn every day and I am thin. Clearly you haven't done your research properly because eating the Skinny brands doesn't automatically make you fat.

JON BRODY

Send a shot of yourself to the Headquarters. I will be the final judge of whether you're thin.

From: Whole Foods Market, Inc.
To: Jon Brody
Subject: Recent Purchase

Dear Jon Brody,

You recently made a purchase at our North Miami Beach, FL store of $412.30 (records indicate it was 25 pounds of imported long grain Italian Rice). The check you paid with has bounced, and we are requesting that you provide an alternative form of payment for $442.30 (the cost of the merchandise plus a $30 bounced check fee). If we do not receive payment in the next 10 business days, we will pursue this matter with our legal department. Please note that your name has been added to the list of customers from whom we can no longer accept checks.

Best regards,
Whole Foods Market, Inc.

THREE

- Buy organic red cabbage (Remember: somewhere other than Whole Foods)

- Check up on Maxi workout and diet routine

- Stretch out hip

- Order Ivy League license plate guard

- Order frozen Sardines

- Shave legs

- Industrial steamer — call customer support

- Refill public library print card for new book pages

- Investigate time-share farmland plot

cakeluver

❤ 25 likes

cakeluver Just completed 80% of my to-do list. Cupcakes for a reward!

lvnglgndry @CakeLuver reward yourself with a workout

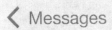

Messages **Ma** Contact

Hi honey! Can you pick up some paper towel and wax paper.

Sure Ma

And some tin foil. I'm making roast sausage tonight.

Ok

But you know I don't eat that.

Well, you'll have a taste. You're still living in my house so you don't have a choice.

Btw, the Ashcrofts will be joining us.

Please not tonight. Mr. Ashcroft talks so loud and stays really late every time he comes.

LivingLegendaryBlog.com

Do More, Say Less

There's a saying at the Living Legendary Headquarters: "Do more, say less." The next time you go out to dinner or for a drink, pay close attention to the people around you. They will likely be conversing with enthusiasm, fully animated, and completely engaged. Living Legends exert themselves to full capacity *during the day*, and so by night fall, they are thoroughly wiped out — without an ounce of energy to utter a single word. The folks prancing around at night, talking for hours on end probably aren't worth listening to. Ideally, you should be socializing with other Living Legends anyway — none of whom will be found in a venue after sunset because they're at home, recovering for the next day. General consensus: there's no excuse for being out at night. If you happen to find *yourself* out and fully energized, you're falling short in Living Legendary.

If you feel like you're missing out by declining your new friend's invitation to drinks, simply seek out those people you would have interacted with at night and ask for their book to read *during the day*. In this way, you can directly access whatever valuable thoughts or discussions they harbor — and get yourself some extra sleep in the process. If you discover they haven't written a book, then they probably don't have anything significant to say anyway. You'll have in turn saved yourself many vapid evenings.

COMMENTS (1)

SOCIALITE

Hello Jon, I have been exploring your site and I am quite intrigued with your "Living Legendary" as you put it. While many of the concepts you proselytize I agree with, such as organic diet, focus, and 100 percent effort, there are several that I disagree with, and some I find quite alarming. First, it seems the lifestyle choices and behavior you teach are anti-social. In one of your videos, you say pick-up basketball games and team sports with other individuals will result in injury. In another video, you go among the "nightlife," as you put it, and comment that it's a "primitive jungle" and a "waste of time." In this post, you mention that socializing in the evening isn't useful. In another post, you say that those who aren't "Living Legendary" aren't worth being around. This kind of elitist attitude, in my opinion, can be regressive socially, professionally, and emotionally. In your website video, "Live Like a Spartan and Start Living Legendary," you seem to enjoy a minimalist living style. This is a lifestyle I can relate to, and actually agree with given the sensationalism of media, television, and American society more generally. But sleeping on the floor? Furnishing your apartment with exclusively upright chairs? Rubbing beet juice on your face in the middle of the night (by the way, is that really healthy)? All of this seems borderline extreme. I guess my question is, how do you find a fine balance between having an active social life, and "Living Legendary?"

From: Jon Brody
To: Deborah Shuckman
Subject: Materials

Dear Ms. Shuckman,

I mailed you the materials (manuscript along with the proposal) at your request several weeks ago. Have you received them? If so, have you had a chance to take a look?   Thank you and I look forward to hearing from you. Jon Brody

From: Jon Brody
To: Susan Ashcroft
Subject: Fwd: RE: Living Legendary

Dear Mrs. Ashcroft,

It was a pleasure having dinner with you on Saturday night, and I want to thank you again for putting me in touch with Mr. Illuminet. Like you said, Mr. Illuminet is very impressive — it's incredible someone could make enough money from a career in journalism to become a top financier of the Republican Party. (As a side note, I was curious: how does such a staunch Republican have so many influential Democratic friends — Bill Clinton, John Kerry, Rahm Emanuel, etc.?) Mr. Illuminet wrote back to me today, and I've attached his email below... was interested to hear your thoughts on his advice. Do you think I should probe further about potential routes for publication? Given what he wrote, I think he's intimating the book won't appeal to young people. Thanks again.

Jon Brody

From: Ron Illuminet, CEO AllNews.com
To: Jon Brody
Subject: RE: Living Legendary

Jon,

Thanks for passing along your resume as well as your Living Legendary manuscript which I glanced through last night. Seems to me you would be a nice fit for a publication like Esquire, GQ, men's health, or fitness... those publications that are more targeted to young men. AllNews.com is focused on the 50+ baby boomer audience, probably more concerned with retirement issues than, let's say, reaching a 3% body fat. But it appears as though you're very knowledgable about lifestyle topics that would be much in tune with certain publications editorially, or maybe even on television. You should think about beginning your career with one of these publications, but then start brainstorming ways to become involved with film or television, as I think that's where the bigger money is and more career openings. Possibly if you tried to get an internship, you might benefit from working at one of these publications and then you can show them your manuscript of the types of subjects you're interested in. In a general sense young people don't buy books of this sort. It's a generational thing, especially with the Internet now... What exactly is your intended market? Is it young males who want to lose weight and become romantic? Are you aiming to tap into the organic produce market? Are you looking to promote a lifestyle brand? I'm a bit confused about what you're trying to accomplish because the scope is so wide... maybe you need to focus yourself more, especially at the outset. Women are very much interested in nutrition and exercise, so they actually might be a great target but you need an execution plan on what you would want to do... There's a young man who wrote a book on exercise and he became very famous in his 20s. I think he is a Latino guy and he wrote a book about exercising 12 minutes a day... His name may re-enter my mind at some point, but he could be an excellent model for you in terms of your business approach... I wish you great success! Best, Ron

From: Susan Ashcroft
To: Jon Brody
Subject: Re: Fwd: RE: Living Legendary

Ask him to mentor you. Cc to me
Sent from my iPhone

LivingLegendaryBlog.com

Coffee Drinkers

Living Legends live addiction-free lives. If they are "addicted," it's always to something good — hard exercise, nutritious food, proper sleep, regular sex, etc. Coffee drinking is a silent, widespread, and dangerous addiction that has been overlooked by our modern society. Nobody perceives the eight-cup-a-day-er as unhealthy or as having any pressing lifestyle issues to address.

Yet any way you look at it, coffee drinkers are completely dependent on their substance. Without their morning cup, they would cease to function. Coffee drinkers go through life on an artificial high, thoroughly detached from their baseline psychological state, and, in turn, their true personality. They take on mundane tasks, bland Excel spreadsheets, and mind-numbing errands with ferocity, vigor, and excitement, all the while singing the "Heigh Ho" chant in unison. Peppy, upbeat, and 100% positive, there's no stopping coffee drinkers from taking on the world once they've made it through Hump Day.

Strip the coffee and what do you have? A tired, cranky, unproductive, unresponsive corpse that likely couldn't drive to work, let alone wake up. And once you're on the stuff, you're on it for life because it would take years to regain the energy to make it through the day naturally. While coffee will certainly "wake you up," it will also make you devastatingly tired if you don't intake your daily prescription. (Coffee doesn't actually wake you up, it *puts you to sleep* because you're living a life detached from a "sober" state.)

Coffee drinkers are usually alcoholics, because you can't have one without the other. The coffee wakes you up, and the alcohol puts you to sleep — removing any need for natural biological processes. Hell, might as well spare the body of having to function at all by adding in some Pepto-Bismol, Dulcolax, Ambien, and Viagra to the mix. In the end, it's better for everyone isn't it? Your body can take it easy while the drugs, alcohol, and coffee companies reel in billions. A formula for all-around success.

COMMENTS (1)

DARK ROAST

I drink several cups of coffee every day and feel great. In fact, "great" doesn't even begin to describe how good I feel from it. To say coffee is addicting and dangerous is ludicrous. Plus, studies have shown it's good for you.   For anyone following this blog, I urge you to do your own research and stop listening to this maniac. There's no basis behind what he's saying, the guy is just rambling.

From: Deborah Shuckman
To: Jon Brody
Subject: RE: Materials

Dear Jon,

Thank you for submitting to us. I was interested in the idea of your book because I compete in cross-country skiing races, so I interact with people who have your diligent attidude about exercise and health all the time. Unfortunately, we cannot take on your title. I personally do not enjoy the tone of the book and the character of yourself that you are creating. I respect your decision to be a sort of Gordon Ramsay character for exercise and health, but this is not the type of character that I like to take advice from. I also found many of your perspectives (and the way you went about describing them) a bit unpalatable. If you would like for me to be more specific, please let me know.

Take care,

Deborah Shuckman

From: Jon Brody
To: Deborah Shuckman
Subject: RE: RE: Materials

Deborah,

I'm disappointed you had this reaction. I was sincerely hoping we could work together. Of course, send along whatever specifics you have — any feedback is helpful at this point. I will query you shortly with my second book — ANIMAL FARM: A 21st CENTURY REDUX — an extension of Orwell's classic examining the effects of our modern food culture in detail (specifically why the "farm animals" aren't the livestock anymore). It will be a few more months before it's complete, but stay on the lookout. Thanks for your time. Jon Brody

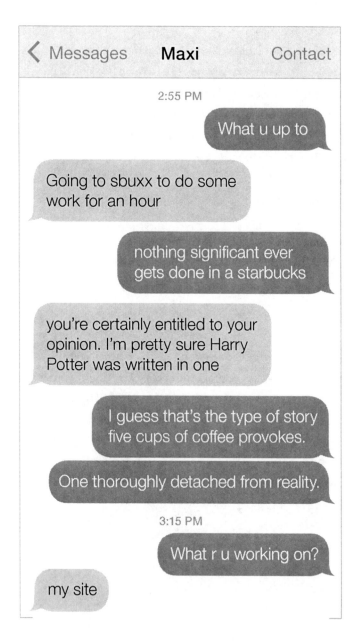

Messages   **Maxi**   Contact

2:55 PM

What u up to

Going to sbuxx to do some work for an hour

nothing significant ever gets done in a starbucks

you're certainly entitled to your opinion. I'm pretty sure Harry Potter was written in one

I guess that's the type of story five cups of coffee provokes.

One thoroughly detached from reality.

3:15 PM

What r u working on?

my site

which one?

the knock-off of Living Legendary?

😡😡 you're not the only one who can be into fitness!

It's a little weird if both of us have a fitness blog tho.

U should come up with something original

you can't trademark a pushup

I was the one who put u on your fitness program in the first place!

I was going to the gym way before we met

but were you wearing the sweatsuit?

I was sweating just fine.

The Living Legendary Framework, Manuscript Preface

Living Legendary entails following your passions, regardless of the immediate outcome or what the outside opinion is. Living Legends are visionaries, pioneers, moguls, and trend-setters — never willing to settle for mediocrity or conform to the status quo.

Take my own path as an example. After graduating from the

Ivy League, I was pushed by those closest to me to take a "real" nine to five job — yet I pushed back by continuing to invest in the Living Legendary Framework. During that time, I reminded myself that I was putting my energy into a long-term project, one that would require many years — likely decades — before it made any money. I had full faith that the Living Legendary movement would eventually catch on. It was never about "if," it was about "when."

I can't say I didn't have my low points. I remember the time I was stationed at a run-down Fedex Office — in one of the most crime-plagued areas of South Florida — pleading with a 350-pound woman, one hand on a photocopier and the other grasping a three-quarters-eaten meatball hero protruding from a torn paper bag, to print and bind my Living Legendary rough draft so I could get it over to the eighty year-old "movie producer" — Earl — at the helm of a locally-run, one-man-show "production" company (the business card dubbed it "Produce with Earl") whom I met at a gas station an hour earlier. Earl informed me he had vast connections with influential creative artists — and while he was definitely suffering from a moderate form of Alzheimer's (me having to repeatedly remind him that it wasn't titled "Laughing Leopards" and targeted towards the feline-obsessed) I wasn't going to pass up a unique opportunity to have my work read.

Despite all of it, I never lost faith. I knew deep down that the Living Legendary Framework was revolutionary — even though I wasn't blessed with the best connections for getting my work out, or an inner circle of family and friends that saw eye to eye. I never blamed anyone, though, because I knew that their perspective was shaped by a much broader social mindset — one that doesn't leave room for following passion if it means you won't walk away with a sizable pay-check. Nobody thought my investments were worth the time or the effort — but I was confident I could overcome their shortsightedness and achieve greatness with my work.

I did benefit from the financial backing of Ma (my mother) during this period. I lived in my childhood house (something your standard self-help guru wouldn't readily admit) and she footed the bill for my daily food expenses. But Ma wasn't happy about the situation, to say the least, and she often threatened to "hit [me] with the ugly stick," or worse, cut me off and "throw [me] onto the street where I belonged." She wanted me to stop "wasting my time" and do something productive with myself ("book writing isn't productive, Ma?" I would often ask). Ma advised I "stop this Living Legendary bull crap before it alienates everyone and makes you friendless." (By that point, I had only one friend left anyway — Jerry — a pal from middle-school who had become clinically insane after a routine tooth implant procedure punctured a neurological nerve).

Ma would constantly reiterate "You're not a visionary," and I'll be forthright in saying there was a brief period when I debated abandoning the book writing to set up an online shop for fitness trinkets (at Ma's recommendation). The site would sell Nike fuel bands, sunglasses, yoga mats, headphones, moisture-wicking socks, and water bottle-belts. But soon after, I regained my senses and pushed ahead. I finished the first book and rode the momentum forward by organizing a plan for the second. As I sat down to begin the new introduction, I heard a knock on my door, and Ma entered with a plate of brownies, wanting to know what I was doing.

"I'm writing another book. I just finished organizing it," I informed her.

Ma gave me a blank, angry look, and turned to leave the room. A second later she whipped herself around and said: "No, honey. Please don't do that anymore."

Living Legendary means having faith in your potential, and never backing down. It's normal to have moments of doubt along the way. I certainly did. "What if people really don't want to become Living Legends?" I would often ask myself late at night. "Or even worse, mistakenly believe they already are?"

I was motivated to part from Ma's britches, and so I started to brainstorm ways I could generate income on the side but not abandon my primary focus. The only feasible option seemed to become a porn actor, scenes taking place for a maximum of one hour and me walking away with a respectable sum. Was my plus-sized member the only money-generating asset I had left? At that time, most likely. But that didn't mean I couldn't use my faithful companion to do away with Ma, live on my own, and pave the way for megastardom.

I had tea with Ms. Flippinsteel today. She asked about you.

That's good. Send my regards.

She can't understand what you're doing with yourself. She always had such high regard for you, and then with the Ivy League.

Has something changed?

Well, she said she thinks you're selling yourself short.

I'm not. I'm doing the best thing I can.

Honey. I'm not sure about that.

Really, I'm not sure.

> It doesn't matter! Don't you get it?
> I don't care about Ms. Flippinsteel,
> Cathy Benedict, the Ashcrofts, or
> anyone else around here.

> You included.

> Just forget what anyone else
> says. I don't want to hear it
> and you shouldn't either.

LivingLegendaryBlog.com

The Road Trip

The American road trip is a Legend-killing pastime. This premise of driving around *for fun* — when you don't actually need to go somewhere — is completely alien to the productive, optimized lifestyle that Living Legends aspire to. And the problem with the road trip doesn't just stem from the wasted time rolling around aimlessly — it has as much to do with the physical damage that the participants accrue. Folks who reason they're "on the open road" fail to realize they're actually in the closed car, confined in uncomfortable positions for extended periods of time with limited movement, provoking stiffness in every joint and muscle of the body. Let's put it this way: nobody is popping out of their vehicle after passing through multiple states and heading into a Legendary, three-hour workout.

Moreover, the road trip is integrally intertwined with eating…the most unhealthy food possible. Road-trippers fuel themselves and their cars during various "pit stops," snacking on chips, Oreos, Slim Jims, Twinkies, soda, and whatever else they can get their hands on. When diabetes-inducing munchies aren't enough, fast food restaurants are the go-to, whichever one happens to be closest to the highway. Several hundred miles in, road-trippers no longer have a choice regarding what they eat — unless you consider deciding between Wendy's and Taco Bell a choice. They are at the mercy of which French fry vendor set up shop just off Exit 334.

The Living Legendary Framework, Book Proposal Similar Titles

1.) WEALTH IS HEALTH by Lishort Pudirich (The Designer Group, 2011). Pudirich posits that owning a $4,000 purse and an Italian sports car is the path to a healthy life. She argues that luxury goods improve self-esteem, confidence, and overall fulfillment — a psychological boost that she claims manifests in real physical benefits and long life. Similar in that both books aim to uncover the secrets behind what constitutes a healthy life; difference is each author's conclusion.

2.) THE THREE-HOUR LIFE by Isym Serris? (The Self-Empowerment Farse, an imprint of Instant Fix With No Fix Books 2013). Serris? isn't just unique in the last character of his name; he proposes a revolutionary approach to population control and self-actualization by arguing that an individual, upon reaching adulthood, can achieve full potential in just three hours (after which he may relieve his strain on the planet's resources by opting to be euthanized). Similar in that both books outline routes for maximizing output, with the difference being the time frames involved. Serris? claims it can be done in three hours; LIVING LEGENDARY argues it takes the full length of a multi-decade life.

3.) ROAD TRIP REFUGES by Wandering Mouthful (The Sitmur Muvliss Press, 2007). Mouthful takes an in-depth look at the "most-appealing" off-road food dives across the United States, recommending that car-goers order at "least three entrée-size dishes per stop" in order to avoid missing out on each location's specialties. Mouthful, a Native American, has embraced the American road trip culture as his own, despite the fact these pathways have cut through his ancestors' formerly-pristine and ecologically-diverse lands. Similar in that Mouthful and I discuss the road trip at length, with the difference being what we advise filling our mouths with.

4.) STAYING PRODUCTIVE WHILE RAISING A PRODUCTIVE CHILD by Theral B. Chrugadix-Anniway (Lenience and Convenience Hardcovers, an outgrowth of the Kelloggs and Dairy Producers of

America Educational Initiative). Chrugadix-Anniway argues that feeding your children pre-packaged, pre-prepared, and easy-to-consume foods — specifically cereals with milk, cereal bars, cereal-based desserts, cheese sticks, and microwavable cheese pizzas — results in optimal productivity for both parent and child, as parents don't waste time in the kitchen and kids obtain five times their recommended daily fat and sugar intake, fully energized from spiked blood sugar and excess glycogen reserves so they can knock out homework assignments and partake in numerous extracurriculars. Similar in that LIVING LEGENDARY deals with productivity and targets the youth, difference being the recommendations themselves.

5.) LET'S TAKE A SHOT WITH THE DEVIL by Trucker Sachs (Misdirected Lifeguides for the Lost, Inc. 2006). A #1 *Temporary Escape Magazine* bestseller with over 110 weeks on the list (second only to WHY YOU SHOULD TAKE A LUXURY VACATION), the book is similar to LIVING LEGENDARY in terms of the targeted audience — difference being that the Living Legendary Framework advocates an opposite path. Sachs presents a life of irresponsibility, carelessness, and lack of health, where hangovers and drunken, unprotected sexual encounters are the gold-standard currency. If Sachs' work — rooted in tales of life-shortening pursuits that provoke fecal incontinence — can tap into the psyches of young people, LIVING LEGENDARY will certainly connect with them too, only with a stronger and more compelling message. The youth of today are looking for — but haven't yet found — a role model who isn't afraid to challenge Sachs and other self-destructive personalities, someone who will probe a bit deeper and ask: "Is this guy really 'cool,' or is he just downright pathetic?"

6.) THE OBESITY IRONY: WHEN SMALLER MEANS SICKER AND BIGGER MEANS HEALTHIER by E. Turcake (The Second Helpings Group, 2013). Turcake argues that you can be "350 pounds, in-shape, and incredibly healthy" — that the "true assassin isn't obesity." Similar in the sense that LIVING LEGENDARY discusses obesity at length; difference being the Living Legendary Framework maintains the contrary viewpoint. THE OBESITY IRONY targets overweight, depressed, sex-starved middle-aged women by telling them it's okay they're fat, and that it's not their fault. LIVING LEGENDARY preaches a realistic doctrine, where gluttony and self-destructive behavior aren't lauded. Whichever side you take, it's clear from all of this that people do want to talk about obesity, and LIVING LEGENDARY will make it crystal clear once and for all that "loving your love handles" is in no way a "route to loving yourself."

From: Jon Brody
To: Trucker Sachs
Subject: Mentor

Dear Trucker,

I have been a fan since reading LET'S TAKE A SHOT WITH THE DEVIL during college. I'm a recent graduate of the Ivy League, and

I've written a book targeting a similar audience as your work, the difference being that my manuscript advocates an opposite lifestyle. Imagine your narrator took a 180 and decided to put his energies into becoming healthy, responsible, and productive. Imagine he became an asset to society, somebody you could actually respect. Based heavily on my own experience, my book — THE LIVING LEGENDARY FRAMEWORK — presents a feasible path for young people to optimize their lives and become what I refer to as a "Living Legend." I'm looking for a mentor to help steer me onto the right course, and I wanted to reach out to see if you might have any interest in getting involved.

Thank you and I hope to hear from you.

Jon Brody

Don't need to send pic. Should just be veggies like I told you

No cheese or bacon like the other day.

Send me a pic of your nipples instead.

haha ok 😍 ☺️

I'm ready to lick them

Suck out some milk while I'm at it

Little extra nutrition never hurts

We don't eat dairy.

The Living Legendary Framework, Manuscript
Chapter 9: Legendary Romance

<u>Lean Down Your Girlfriend</u>

My girlfriend — Maxi — can't understand why I don't want us to sleep in the same bedroom. I assure her it's not about lack of affection, but rather a Living Legend's need to secure restful sleep — which can never be achieved with someone tossing and turning next to you (or worse, snoring). Yet still she has difficulty accepting it.

What idiot came up with the idea that sleeping in the same bed is romantic? How can you be romantic if you're unconscious? Living Legends certainly follow through with romantic evenings, complete with Legendary lovemaking — but then they retire to the second bedroom to recharge for the next day.

There's nothing more important for a Living Legend than proper sleep. If your rest is compromised one night, it will usually take four days to recover. Legends maximize their output every single day — which means there's simply no room for error.

I never want to take a risk that my sleep might be disturbed. And it's not that I didn't try a same-room sleeping arrangement with Maxi, because I did. She goes to the bathroom four times a night. I explained that Living Legends stay hydrated through water-rich foods — *not* by drinking two gallons each day. But the magazines tell her that's how you stay thin, so my input doesn't fully resonate, I suppose.

I can't say Maxi isn't fully responsive to my suggestions, though. See, Maxi is set on getting married and she'll do anything to get a ring on her finger. Living Legends never acquire a wife until they've arrived at Legendary status, yet I've withheld my marital timeframe (another decade before I will have solidified my Legendary rank) from Maxi in order to motivate her fitness-wise. Time and again I've told her: "I'd rather die than see those fat arms walking down the aisle."

Before you start calling Jon Brody a "jerk," you need a little background here. Truth is, Maxi's been thin from the waist down her whole life. She has a lean butt, toned calves, and slender feet. But the way she got there was "calorie restriction," a euphemism for starvation. She wanted to live a life void of both eating and exercise — and she followed through with her strategy for the better half of adulthood. Yet even with suffering in the form of persistent hunger, and despite a successfully skeletal lower half, Maxi's arms have enough meat on them to feed a family of ten. So I said: "Maxi — you want to get married? Then you had better stop starving yourself and start working out so you can get your arms thin. Your current regimen isn't helping you, it's actually *harming* the quality of your life."

She listened. At my request, Maxi now runs twice per day (30 minutes each time) on the grass field outside the Headquarters in 90 degree Florida heat... with two sweatshirts on. She does arm circles while she runs too.

I'm proud of Maxi because, on her own initiative, she added a pair of arm-sleeves to wear underneath the sweatshirts. This was a smart choice on her part because it's her forearms that are in the most need of thinning, and the sleeves seem to target this area perfectly. So far she's been on the program for five months and it has been a success, indicated not so much by her weight loss as the fact she no longer menstruates.

Even though I've been strict with Maxi, she has proven to be a tremendous asset in my own quest to Live Legendary. Of those close to me, Maxi has been the *most* receptive to the Framework, though this may be driven more by her many insecurities than a true, burning desire to become a Legend. But I don't hold this against her. It's those same insecurities that drew me to her in the first place, as I knew I could mold her in the way I saw fit. As a bonus, Maxi has inadvertently become my sole confidant and companion, and having her by my side during the preliminary phases of Framework development has been mentally stabilizing. Not to mention providing me with an image of "normalcy" to the outside world when many have written me off as a lunatic.

I don't worry that Maxi will one day read this because I've already given her a signed copy of the manuscript (without this chapter), which I've fastened with lock and key to her bedside. Maxi's taken enough notes on it by now that she probably could write a full book of Legendary commentary on her own. But we've discussed that the limelight will be mine for now — until Maxi is finally thin and ready to enter the outside world. By that time, Living Legendary will be a phenomenon and so her having a small following of her own won't pose any threat to the franchise.

From: Roy Ramones
To: Jon Brody
Subject: RE: Query

Jon, Thanks for getting in touch. It's an intriguing idea, but it's probably too early for you to be pitching it to agents. You should also consider remaking your similar books list, since your profile is nothing like Pudirich or Sachs. (Pudirich is an internationally-recognized psychology professor, and Sachs was a monster Internet celebrity when he wrote his book.) They may be your inspiration, but their readers are not indicative of your potential market. Somewhere down the road, I'd be happy to reconsider this.

Best, Roy

yea I am man

compared to you I'm obese lol

u went off the diet?

a little bit. I need to get back on track.

I don't know how you do it.

I've been pretty good all year, just recently.

Been eating a lot at the restaurant lol

once you start it's a slippery slope.

When I c u over the holiday I'm gonna walk the other way if you're fat. Pretend I don't know you

lol

LivingLegendaryBlog.com

Breakfast Out

If you find yourself eating breakfast out, you are falling short in becoming a Living Legend. Why? It's not just about the bad food you're eating — and make no mistake, virtually all breakfast restaurant options are unhealthy. It's about the lifestyle it represents — one of laziness and gluttony. If you don't have the energy to throw some oats into a pot of boiling water, it's unlikely you'll have the reserves to follow through with a proper workout — or write a chapter in your new book. If you look closely (or even from a distance), you'll find that those frequenting the local breakfast parlor are singularly unattractive, singularly unproductive, and singularly in need of a pep talk. Living Legends aren't found with a Waffle Sundae peering over the *Sunday Times* — they're in the sun, making the most of their day by getting in an extended workout after a homemade morning meal.

COMMENTS (1)

DAMEON

I think you overgeneralize here. I eat breakfast out on the weekends after I hit the gym, and it hasn't affected my fitness negatively. Brody — I think it's time you quit with this bullshit and get a real job. Nothing is more "unattractive" than living off your parents, no matter how many breakfasts you eat out.

TWEETS	FOLLOWING	FOLLOWERS	FAVORITES	LISTS
412	5K	80K	1,005	3

Tweets   Tweets & replies   Photos & videos

Living Legendary @LvngLgndry · 3h
Eat. Sleep. Edit. Repeat. #YoungDickens #IvyLeague #LivingLegendary

↩ 0   ⟲ 1   ★ 1

NYU Pride 2011 @NYUPride2011 · 3h
Retweet: Eat. Sleep. Edit. Repeat.: @LvngLgndry **Young Dick** #IvyLeagueSucks #GoBobcats #PurpleIsTheNewCrimson

From: Susan Ashcroft
To: Jon Brody
Subject: FWD: FWD: Mentor

Sorry, Jon. I tried.

Sent from my iPhone

From: Ron Illuminet
To: Susan Ashcroft
Subject: FWD: Mentor

Susan, I really don't have time to do this..... His career interests are totally different than AllNews and it's in his best interest to focus on the areas that would assist him in enhancing his career prospects. He appears to be a very nice young man, and will be fine going forward. I'm sure.

Forwarded Message:
From: Jon Brody
To: Ron Illuminet
Subject: Mentor

Dear Mr. Illuminet,

Can you serve as my mentor in this process?

Jon Brody

*   *   *

From: Susan Ashcroft
To: Ron Illuminet
Subject: RE: FWD: Mentor

Ok. Any ideas on a mentor ?

Sent from my iPhone

From: Ron Illuminet
To: Susan Ashcroft
Subject: RE: RE: FWD: Mentor

Well in my opinion I think the best mentor is a job!

Ron Illuminet

Sent from my iPhone

LivingLegendaryBlog.com

Sweat Garments

Living Legendary involves paying attention to which parts of your body are predisposed to weight gain — and then targeting these areas through the use of sweat garments (sweatshirts, sweatpants, leg warmers, arm-sleeves, ski masks, etc.).

During your workouts, you want to raise your body temperature an extra 10 to 15 degrees in your "fatty places" in order to incinerate the excess mass.

When Living Legends work out in the gym (gyms are particularly problematic due to air conditioning) — or in any weather under 90 degrees — they always wear a full sweatsuit in order to keep the core body temperature elevated. But the sweatsuit is just the first piece of the puzzle.

In an instance where a Living Legend is predisposed to weight gain in a particular area of the body, he or she can target this location by implementing additional sweat garments *underneath* the sweatsuit. If it's the legs, use a pair of extra-thick leg warmers. If it's the torso, wrap your midsection in a large bed-sheet or towel, affixed with Saran wrap or masking tape. If it's the face that's particularly bloated, purchase a wool ski mask — no matter if it's the heart of summer (just be sure not to walk into a bank). The idea isn't to look stylish or sexy, or even fit in. There's one focus only: building the Legendary physique.

COMMENTS (2)

JAMIE

I relate to this idea of sweating and often take Bikram Yoga classes.

Do you think sweat clothes are also necessary for hot yoga?

JON BRODY

Yes

The Living Legendary Framework, Manuscript Chapter 8: Establish Your Headquarters. Then Never Leave.

The Annual Restaurant Meal

Living Legends understand how powerful and addicting restaurant and pre-prepared food can be, and therefore make it a point to prepare all of their own meals. Just one single meal at a restaurant will ignite the internal food cravings engine for days, and not even the most strong-willed person can overcome these cravings without eventually giving in.

Eating every meal in your house for months in a row can become tiresome, especially mentally. For this reason, I escape my four walls *once each year* and "enjoy" a meal out at a restaurant. Yet with each annual restaurant meal that passes, I am further convinced that my eat-at-home regimen is the best — indeed, *the only* — option.

As soon as I hit the restaurant strip, I am always overwhelmed by the hoards of people eating there. My eyes immediately begin scanning the surrounding heads, but what I see doesn't seem human — the faces are bloated, swollen, and deformed. Conversations are augmented by the movement of second chins that sway in sync with the mouths opening and closing above them. Clucking, snorting, and slurping accompany the clinking of silverware on cheese-fry plates, along with the crackling of ice cubes as a third refill of Mountain Dew is poured. It's like a carefully-manicured and well-maintained zoo, in which animals are tightly quarantined, and then overfed and forced to stay sedentary for hours in a row. But these "animals" have free will!

I sit down with my company at a local spot that claims to offer "healthy cuisine." It is soon revealed that "healthy" includes brie cheese and "fritters" (fried starch balls). Two magnificently large ladies at the adjacent table — stomachs large enough to rebound a skydiver whose chute fails to eject — merrily down a spread of chili cheese nachos.

We're sitting outdoors, and one of my companions mentions that she's worried about the stray cat wandering around the seating area. She requests to speak with the maitre d' — 5' 9" and well over 350 lbs. Barely able to squeeze through the tightly separated tables, he finally makes it over to us, but doesn't have much knowledge about the cat or any adoption options. It's a humid summer night and he is perspiring profusely, breathing heavily too. We ask him to recommend some dishes, and in this regard he is well-informed, revealing that he eats several plates from the kitchen every night before his shift. Not a good omen for how this food will affect us.

I start to sweat myself, but for a very different reason — I'm brainstorming how to get myself the hell out of here, not offend my company, *and* make it home before the hunger from my 9-mile-per-hour, 35-minute run earlier that evening strips me of consciousness. I excuse myself to use the restroom so I can buy more time and space to think — yet any internal dialogue is cut short the moment I open the door to the dining room. There's a party of twelve, each heavier than the next, aggressively grabbing at an alarmingly large spread at the center table. They're full of energy and laughing jovially, scarfing down fritters two at a time, one young man holding a pair above his head with an outstretched arm before letting gravity do the rest of the work (a scene displaying a striking resemblance to "tea-bagging," which I've been fortunate enough to experience — myself in the position of the fritter, and the "diner" much thinner and much more female). The fat-enriched globules are suspended mid-air for a brief second before his widened mouth hospitably takes them in. It reminds me of a whale-feeding I once watched at Sea World as a young boy.

I won't need to watch any scary movies for the foreseeable future given that this scene will keep me up for many sleepless nights. I resolve to cut my bathroom trip short and head back outside. The maitre d' is still hovering over our table, sweat droplets flowing freely from his forehead — one entering my friend's merlot without her even noticing. I start running... in the opposite direction. Panic-stricken, I push through several valet waist-coats and snatch my own car keys from the cabinet despite protest. I sprint to the parking lot and waste no time turning the ignition. Two minutes later I'm doing ninety on the expressway. I reach into the cooler on the passenger seat floor, always stocked with several New Zealand Braeburns. Ten minutes and two apple cores later, I'm home and downing organic wild rice and fresh vegetables. My company, along with the maitre d', are probably wondering where I am. But it's of no consequence because I won't be dealing with them, a restaurant, or anybody else for another year.

Despite their scarring effects, the annual restaurant meals produce unique relics, the bulk of which are now on exhibition at the Headquarters in a glass case labeled "The Last Supper Display" (due to Jon Brody's belief at the moment each meal was completed that it would be the final one to ever be eaten outside his house). Within that case you can find a framed shot of a nauseous Jon Brody after a 32-ounce rib eye, a pair of chopsticks from a meal so salty it necessitated two weeks recovery time, a soiled napkin from a rack of ribs that provoked an immediate five-pound weight gain, and a crumpled $186.58 receipt from a two-person dinner at which all main course offerings were "specials," and so prices hadn't been revealed up front.

From: Eleanor Sanscrit
To: Jon Brody
Subject: RE: Query

Dear Jon,
Your book sounds interesting to me; I like the concept behind it and want to take a closer look. Please do send the full submission. I do need to say up front that the title is not working for me. Is there flexibility there? Many thanks, Eleanor Sanscrit

From: Jon Brody
To: Eleanor Sanscrit
Subject: RE: RE: Query

Ms. Sanscrit,

Thanks for your response and I'm excited you have an interest in the project! I am flexible with the title so long as it includes some variation of the words "live" and "legend." I've attached the full submission and look forward to hearing back from you. Best regards,

Jon Brody

The Living Legendary Framework, Book Proposal Marketing Plan

The LIVING LEGENDARY website (LivingLegendaryBlog.com), blog, Instagram, Twitter (@lvnglgndry), and YouTube channels are all active and growing. But the social media component is only one piece of the marketing plan.

We have the critical opportunity to be the first to bring the phrase LIVING LEGENDARY into the dialogue of daily life. This has the potential to be a distinct marker that stands for health, productivity, and a maximized lifestyle. Using the hashtag #LivingLegendary in social media will begin to power the spread of the phrase. I have already been using this hashtag — online and in local graffiti — and it is catching on with followers.

Beyond hashtags, I plan to use this first LIVING LEGENDARY book as the start of an entire lifestyle brand, delving deeper into each of the Living Legendary components with diet, nutrition, and exercise products, along with follow-up books to extend the brand.

I am in the beginning stages of developing an iPhone app to "gamify" Living Legendary, in which an online community will compete to become *The* Living Legend (a user amasses points through Legendary behavior — which in turn motivates others to do the same). I am also developing a pitch for a television reality show — a pilot presentation will be released shortly on YouTube, and I am hoping to pitch the show to producers to coordinate with the book launch.

In terms of promotional avenues, ambitious high school and college students are the sweet spot for LIVING LEGENDARY. My experience as an Ivy League college athlete gives me insight into how to reach other student athletes in unexpected ways — utilizing online groups and social networks that I am connected with, or touring college athletic departments as a guest instructor to promote the book and the LIVING LEGENDARY framework. I have the credibility few other authors in this space have to reach these student-athletes and, in the process, sell books.

LIVING LEGENDARY makes being healthy, fit, productive, and smart seem cool — and aims to start a new wave of thinking for the youth of today. I plan to reach out for support and endorsements from high school and college authorities.

From: Doug Trimball
To: Jon Brody
Subject: Yesterday's Talk

Jon,

Wanted to send you a quick note about yesterday. First of all, we all appreciate you taking the time to come. I think the class enjoyed having you, but I'm concerned about you continuing to lecture to high school students in this way. I know your "Living Legendary" message has a good intention, but it seems you've veered a bit to the extreme. Telling kids that "Americans are like a fattened herd of cattle ready for the slaughter," that all of our nationally-produced food options are void of nutrition, and that the only way to circumvent obesity is to "import grains from Europe" (how do you even afford that?) seems a bit farfetched, and, in my opinion, unproductive. I fear that if you pursue these talks to a larger degree and impart these philosophies to more young students, the results could prove harmful. These kids are doing their best and I think what you're saying could be more forgiving and provide a bit more leeway. Good luck with your pursuits and hope you have success.

Coach Trimball

‹ Notes

Living Legendary App/ Gamifying Living Legendary

- Users acquire currency for Legendary behavior.

- Annual contest in which five "Living Legends" are declared, with one ultimate winner at the top of the leaderboard. The prize for the five is to trail Jon Brody during a one week period, joining him for organic meals. The winner will be able to opt in for a six-month apprenticeship with Brody, living full-time at the Headquarters.

- Legendary currency acquisition, values (highest to lowest): > 6 months eating meals exclusively at home, > 1 month eating 100% organic food, workout with > 1 liter sweat production (users will have to wring wet clothes into a measuring cup), > 10 hours/night sleep, > 30 minutes stretching, > 2 hour massage, > 2 hours extreme hunger before eating (how to quantify "extreme hunger?")

- Can earn currency by positively influencing others' Legendary behavior: slapping a colleague's morning doughnut to the ground, breaking into random homes and emptying cupboards of Oreos, cheese puffs, and potato chips, slipping sleeping pills into a friend's drink early Saturday evening to prevent him from participating in nightlife, puncturing a family member's tires before he or she was planning to have dinner out, upping your apartment's temperature to 100 degrees so your roommate sweats profusely during house chores, etc.

- The inherent problem with Fitbit and other fitness trackers is that they measure quantity, not quality (total steps vs. pace). Living Legendary app should measure quality — need to figure a quantifiable mechanism for measurement. One possible route could be a Living Legendary-branded heart-rate monitor that ties into the app, where a user only amasses fitness points at HR > 170.

- Think through other gadgets to supplement app: a sensor that attaches to dishwasher to measure how many times per week it runs (a gauge of whether a person is preparing meals at home), a small mouth implant that monitors pesticide and preservative levels (to determine if a person is eating natural, organic foods), a toilet device with a direct feed into the app that analyzes solid waste (so users won't be able to lie about what they eat), etc.

- Possible dating component to app: your matches are determined by how much Legendary currency you've acquired, so "wealthier" users can connect with those of similar status. This will incentivize Legendary behavior because those who are "richer" will naturally be hotter.

LivingLegendaryBlog.com

The Insulating Layer

Living Legendary entails working consistently to shed what Legends refer to as the "insulating layer." This is the layer of excess glycogen stores that accumulate throughout the body — in the muscles and fatty tissue. When you don't work out each day to burn off your insulating layer, the layer steadily accumulates. Years (or decades) of failing to shed the insulating layer results in a fully insulated individual — by tens or hundreds of layers (think Matryoshka doll). The clinical term for these people is "obese."

Living Legends are lean, athletic, and insulation-free — a physical state that only comes about through a consistent routine of rigorous exercise, in which the insulating layer is shed daily.

What happens if you don't shed the insulating layer? Insulation. You will feel uncomfortable. You will smell like body odor (when you fail to expel heat by working out, your body seeks to rid it through the armpits). You will appear generally disagreeable to those around you. The best way to tell if you've shed your insulating layer is to ask yourself: Have I sweated through my clothes today? Follow that up with: Have I sweated through my clothes every day for the last ten years? If you answer in the negative to either of these questions, it's likely your insulating layer hasn't been properly addressed.

If it's under 110 degrees and you're perspiring, you are insulated. Start doing something about it.

From: Trucker Sachs
To: Jon Brody
Subject: RE: Mentor

Jon,

I would be willing to help you in some way. What exactly did you have in mind? My days are pretty jam-packed but I'll see what I can do.

Trucker

From: Jon Brody
To: Trucker Sachs
Subject: RE: RE: Mentor

Trucker,

Thank you! This is incredible news. Would you be able to read a few segments of my book and give some feedback? Specifically how to make it more appealing to agents/editors. I'm facing a bit of a roadblock in making my work seem appealing to trade publishers.

Jon

From: Trucker Sachs
To: Jon Brody
Subject: RE: RE: RE: Mentor

Sure thing. Send it along.

Trucker

From: Squarespace, Inc.
To: Jon Brody
Subject: LivingLegendaryBlog.com

Dear Mr. Brody,

This is a courtesy email to inform you that your credit card has been declined for this month's billing cycle. According to our records, this is this third month you have missed payment. If you fail to meet your obligations in full by the end of this month, your website will become inactive and your account will be filed with our collections agency.

Best,

The Squarespace Team

LivingLegendaryBlog.com

Hibernation Mode

Living Legends understand that the only way to have a true gauge on the exact amount of food you need is by exercising regularly. Those who don't exercise regularly live their days in what Legends refer to as "hibernation mode." Hibernation mode entails eating meals without fully expending the energy that is coming into the body from the food. Without exercise, the body does not have a gauge on how many calories need to be replaced in the system and *what type* of calories they should be (for instance, whether you need a piece of fish or a piece of fruit). After a three-hour workout, for example, a Living Legend will eat roughly the same portion size as someone sitting next to him who has done no exercise. This is because a Legend's body has adapted to expending the energy from food in an efficient and effective manner. The person next to him, on the other hand, is hibernating and storing excess calories.

The only way to overcome your appetite is to burn off your caloric intake through rigorous workouts. There is a saying, "Athletes eat and train, not exercise and diet." Whether you're an athlete or not, you need to be eating and "training" (working out). The workouts will serve as an appetite suppressant and prevent the overconsumption of food.

COMMENTS (2)

CHARLES

Over the past six months, I've been facing constant fatigue and often find myself sleeping upwards of fifteen hours per day. I stumbled across your blog and noticed this post. How does sleeping a lot relate to this concept of "hibernation mode?" I exercise once per week.

JON BRODY

Sleeping upwards of fifteen hours per day indicates depression more than hibernation — and this seems like the most logical diagnosis given your once-per-week exercise schedule. But I wouldn't be the one to advise here, I'm expert in a different arena. You should seek out an M.D. — he or she will be able to prescribe you some medication.

Cardboardmag.com/Living_Legendary_Doubles_ Audience

The Living Legendary blog has doubled its audience in the last three months to a staggering 1 million page views. But as a significant slab of the Internet flocks to Brody's site, we can't help but question the legitimacy of his propositions. Brody coins his own terms with respect to exotic fitness and diet claims — the "Insulating Layer," and "Hibernation Mode" — and posits that "Skinny" brand products don't make you thin. Yet without any formal certifications (Cardboard Mag did an extensive background check which revealed nothing), people are starting to wonder: should they be reading this blog for the content, or the entertainment value?

The Living Legendary Framework, Manuscript Chapter 11: Legendary Nutrition

Pursue a Sustainable Nutritional Path

It's not by chance that health-conscious people today aren't sure what to eat. The widespread confusion over nutrition-related issues — whether concerning carbohydrates, egg yolks, protein, avocado, sugary foods, oils, diet soda, or supplements — is manufactured by food, diet, health, and nutritional supplement companies *themselves*… on purpose. They don't want you to know for certain what to eat and what not to, because if you did then they wouldn't be able to sell you a new fad diet each year, manipulate sales to match variations in production, and market cheap and unhealthy food under the guise of being healthy (all of which profits companies heavily while keeping consumers in the dark). Food manufacturers get you to focus on a single nutritional positive of a product — usually matching the momentary fad of "low carb" or "sugar free" — while all other qualities of that food product are negative. As one example, think about the "Fiber One Bar" ad campaign promoting the product's (you guessed it) fiber content. No matter how much fiber you're getting, "Fiber One" is nothing more than a glorified candy bar. Living Legendary involves tackling your eating habits from the ground up in a sustainable and logical manner. This doesn't mean periodically starving yourself, latching on to the latest diet trend, or going on week-long juice cleanses.

Cold-pressed juice companies make it seem like they're offering a solution to the modern day diet conundrum, yet the "food" path they offer is unsustainable over the long haul. Living Legendary means eating your food and drinking water (only water — no soda, vitamin water, or sports drinks) alongside it because no matter how many juice concoctions you down, you can never survive on juice alone. There's a reason we use the word "living" in Living Legendary: Living Legends don't die from starvation — and if they do, they certainly don't pretend like they were fully-satiated in the process.

Mentioning that you "eat" anything other than juice inside your local cold-pressed shop will render you an outcast in seconds. Discussing the eating of real food in the land of juice-goers is like telling a first date you "want to fuck" over a candle-lit dinner at a fancy restaurant. Both admissions would be offensive and out of line in their respective environments.

Nevertheless, the unspoken dialogue runs hard in juicers' minds — just like it does in those (the man's, certainly) on the romantic date. But instead of, "Will she have sex with me tonight?" — in juice land it's, "Will this woman be consuming anything other than that 16 oz cup for the day?" Everyone's dying to get answers, but nobody can verbalize the matter outright. To do so would break the social code and result in embarrassment for all those involved. So what ends up happening? Just like the good-intentioned (nothing wrong with him expecting some action) gentleman footing the $200 lobster dinner without getting laid, those following the path of juice become disappointed, disillusioned, and generally unfulfilled (not to mention, "hangry") without ever being able to voice or discuss these sentiments for fear of being ostracized.

Another instance of this type of unspoken dialogue is during a consultation with a new dietician... realizing upon introduction that he or she is *obese*. While most will recognize the irony, a majority won't verbalize their concerns outright or question the legitimacy of this "professional" for fear of being labeled the equivalent of a racist. Living Legends will have no trouble recognizing (with spoken words, if necessary) that an obese dietician is a quack. It's the same as a "fisherman" who flipped through a pamphlet on how to fish, but who never actually caught one himself, or a "shoemaker" who read a manual on how to go about making a shoe, but who never spent a single day in the workshop.

lvnglgndry
7-Eleven

♥ 64 likes

lvnglgndry A well-marketed candy bar. The staff
at StrengthBar creative certainly knows how
to put a cover over your eyes **#livinglegendary**
#deception #candy

fitobsessed @lvnglgndry are there any bars you can at all recommend? Kind bar? A brand of protein bars? Sometimes I need a quick snack in a package, wondering if any are at all healthy

lvnglgndry @fitobsessed it's called "banana"

thetriathlete3 Actually these aren't bad for events over 30 miles. Wafers are easier to digest than a bar, and endurance puts a lot of strain on the stomach. I do these and fig newtons for races and runs 50k and over, and down a cup of chicken broth at rest stations for potassium.

lvnglgndry @thetriathlete3 well that explains why you're the most out-of-shape "triathlete" I've ever seen. I can guarantee that no champion ironman is downing chicken soup at rest stations.

thetriathlete3 @lvnglgndry You have no idea what you're saying. Your whole blog/instagram/twitter is a sham. I'm a fitness and nutrition specialist and consultant

lvnglgndry @thetriathlete3 YOU are a fitness consultant? That's a joke. You're fat

thetriathlete3 @lvnglgndry I'm getting my PhD in Clinical Nutrition. I work out at an obesity clinic — virtually all of my clients have BMIs over 40, and >40% Body Fat.

lvnglgndry @thetriathlete3 so if you're obese then you're qualified to assist the morbidly obese. Makes a lot of sense

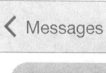

Messages **Maxi** Contact

Did you see the pic?? Is this how I should be cooking?!! 🥖🍅🥒🥒 🍎🍴😋😋

yup looks good. but get rid of those sauces.

That's not tartar sauce is it?

Cuz if it is we're gonna need an intervention.

All veggies should be eaten plain.

ok. Lol yea it's tartar sauce.

I'll throw it out.

good

Pretty soon I'll be able to cook for u too!

They do say the way to a man's heart is through his stomach

the way to my heart is through your ass

From: Jon Brody
To: Eleanor Sanscrit
Subject: RE: RE: Query

Dear Ms. Sanscrit,

Just wanted to touch base and see if you've gotten a chance to look at the book. Thank you. Best regards, Jon Brody

From: Eleanor Sanscrit
To: Jon Brody
Subject: RE: RE: RE: Query

Jon — please go ahead and present to others. We have had a death at the agency and are a bit discombobulated as a result…needing to reassign tasks and, well, recover from the sudden shock.
All the best to you, E.S.

From: Jon Brody
To: Eleanor Sanscrit
Subject: RE: RE: RE: RE: Query

Sorry to hear that. Does that mean you haven't looked at the materials? Jon

juicegirl

♥ 28 likes

juicegirl It's totally ok to drink your dinner! **#kale #parsley #ginger #smoothie**

lvnglgndry If you're drinking your dinner you're anything but ok. You're severely misguided, and likely obese

> **juicegirl** What?! Who the hell are you? Stop commenting on my page
>
> **lvnglgndry** Piece of advice: there's no way you can be drinking meals and following through with Legendary workouts.

From: Jon Brody
To: Juice-Press Weight Loss, Inc.
Subject: Part Replacement

Hello,

I purchased one of your products online two months ago and the clamp recently snapped in half. While I do use the machine every day to make fresh sardine juice (your model is particularly effective in extracting liquid from bones), I take excellent care of it and so this should not have happened. Would it be possible to send a replacement? It's #13aa on the parts list. Thank you.

Jon Brody.

The Living Legendary Framework, Manuscript Chapter 4: Thinking Objectively

The Danger of Denial

My cousin Amy — now in her early thirties — suffered from the sudden onslaught of body hair growth at the age of twenty-one. Every year the family convened for the holidays, new follicles of thick, dark hair had sprouted up on Amy's arms, hands, back, chin, and upper lips. It was clear to me that Amy was getting hairier, and I assumed Amy was aware of it too. I had hoped one year I would show up to a family gathering, and Amy would have dealt with her issue.

It wasn't until Amy was covered to the point of looking like a distant human ancestor that I realized she was in complete denial about her hair growth. We were out to dinner one night at a popular restaurant in Chicago. Even though it was mid-July, Amy was wearing a long sleeve shirt and a scarf that covered her neck, which, at this late stage of her transformation (the hair growth had extended down her chin to her collar bone), she was wearing consistently at social gatherings and evening affairs. We had finished the meal and a gap in conversation prompted Amy to remove her scarf, roll up her sleeves, and look me square in the eye: "Jon, I think I'm getting hairier." Whether this epiphany had occurred around that time, or whether Amy simply hadn't been able to voice her concerns until that moment, it was clear that she was in denial. While the hair growth process had been underway for nearly a decade, it took Amy years to admit it.

Over the course of the next several years, I have observed how Amy has dealt with her issue. The first step was regular waxing appointments, but due to sensitive skin and rapid hair regrowth, all this resulted in was rashes and stubble. Amy then tried laser hair removal, but either due to a faulty job or her hair's continued stubborness, she still suffered from patches in the most problematic areas. Finally, Amy visited a hormone specialist who prescribed a regimen of estrogren supplements, which, after some tweaking over a year period, finally reversed the hair growth.

The reason that Amy's hair growth plight is relevant here is that it represents a consequence of failing to think objectively and tackle your problems head on — two pillars that all Legends adhere to.   Amy simply could not face the situation until the problem had become far too obvious to ignore. Had Amy been able to come to terms right away with her problem, she would have been able to deal with it at the outset. Instead, she suffered through years of embarrassment, mid-summer scarf-wearing, and attempts to convince herself of a reality other than the one that was actually happening.

Amy's story illustrates the lesson: no matter how much you want to believe that something is different than it actually is, the longer the reality will continue to persist. If you are monitoring your weight, step onto a scale. If a term paper deadline is fast approaching, look at a calendar and make a plan. If you have credit card debt, create a schedule for paying it off. Now, not later. Whether numbers on a scale or follicles on your body, you must accept reality and deal with it in an objective way. To Live Legendary, there is no room for denial.

From: Michael Brody
To: Jon Brody
Subject: Book

Jon,

I've made more headway through the book and you're going to need to take out the "Danger of Denial" discussion with Amy (a.k.a. Lisa), as it depicts her in an incredibly negative light, not to mention revealing

private medical procedures and consultations. I'll send you a note once
I've read more. Talk soon,   Your Dad

From: Jon Brody
To: Michael Brody
Subject: RE: Book

Dad, Don't take Amy's, Uncle Larry's, or anyone else's story too
seriously. I'm just using these anecdotes to help the reader understand
the main points. It's not about Amy and her hair problem, or Larry and
his diet smoothies — that's all just characters and stories. The points
I'm trying to make are much more important. In any case, I've already
begun seeing some traction with agents. With some luck, the book
should be on shelves soon. Jon

From: Samuel Gross
To: Jon Brody
Subject: RE: Query

Jon, I'd read your manuscript, but only do that on an exclusive basis, so
you need to decide if that works for you. I don't want to take the time
unless you are committed if I am. Samuel Gross

From: Jon Brody
To: Samuel Gross
Subject: RE: RE: Query

Mr. Gross, Thanks for getting back to me. I've already been in touch
with several agents who are in the process of reviewing my materials —
so I would not be able to afford you exclusive privileges. Let me know
if you would still like to see the manuscript and I will send it. Thanks.
Jon Brody

From: Samuel Gross
To: Jon Brody
Subject: RE: RE: RE: Query

Only on an exclusive basis. Sorry.

I'm thinking of your derierre

?? 😑 😑

I want to put more than a finger in it...

once we're married

how about once we agree to get married

do you mean an engagement?

no a verbal agreement

no way! not more than a finger until I have a ring 💍 📿

well no ring until those arms are lean

From: Cassandra Wile
To: Jon Brody
Subject: Follow Up

Hi Jon: From our discussion, it sounds like we should file an
application for LIVING LEGENDARY in connection with:
Class 25: clothing (we will have to list out the specific items, but we
can append your tagline, "Linens for the Lean" in conjunction with the
mark. Obtaining exclusive rights to a clothing line that only offers waist
sizes 29 and down will prove a bit more problematic, though)
Class 16: series of books on the topic of health, fitness, lifestyle coaching
Class 41: restaurant services
Additionally, it is always a good idea to do a comprehensive search
to see if there are any third parties using the mark. I already did a
preliminary search and found nothing, but we always recommend a
full search to have a better idea of whether there are users out there that
haven't filed yet and who could then interfere with your use later on.

One final note: You mentioned that you were interested in various
iterations of LIVING LEGENDARY — LIVE LEGENDARY, LIVING
LEGEND, LIVING LEGENDARY HEADQUARTERS etc. From a
trademark and branding perspective, this is not ideal (at least not
yet). First, you would technically need to file 2 separate applications,
which is a needless expenditure. Second, when creating a brand and a
trademark consistency of use is very important. Maybe after the mark
has become well known you can use it in different formats, but for now
you should proceed with one version.
Please let me know how you would like to proceed.
Cassandra Wile, Senior Counsel

LivingLegendaryBlog.com

Don't Be a Sheep

Living Legendary means securing your health at all costs, even if that means turning a few heads in the process. When I bring my own container of organic food to social gatherings, my company always raises their eyebrows. When I'm wearing a full sweatsuit at the gym and puddling the floor, those around me give the eye. But in the end, it's of no consequence because I'm doing what's right. Under no circumstances do Living Legends become sheep.

When it comes down to it, the majority conform. They don't want to cause a stir. They're embarrassed by the (negative) attention. They want to fit in and go with the flow. Nothing better represents this than the use of body scanners at airport security checkpoints. It has been well documented that these scanners cause cancer. Yet people walk through them not only willingly, but joyfully. I see elderly women and middle-aged men raising their hands in perky, energetic fashions, looking towards TSA employees for some twisted form of approval — for some short-lived nod of assurance that they are valued, worthwhile members of society. Travelers can avoid going through the body scanners by "opting out," and in place given a manual body search and pat down. I rarely see these pat downs being performed. Why? People don't want to cause a stir, or inconvenience TSA guards at the checkpoint (who often purposefully intimidate travelers to avoid having the extra work of a manual search). These folks are putting politeness ahead of health — a choice no Living Legend would ever make.

The Living Legendary Framework, Manuscript Chapter 13: Legendary Focus

Don't Have an "Experience"

Living Legendary requires a continuous stream of hard work, persistence, and resolve that — when combined over a long-term period of time — produces the Living Legend. Each learning block and each conquered obstacle are cumulative, and they feed off of one another to bring the aspiring Legend progressively closer to his end goal.

Too often you hear people isolating moments in their life — reflecting on them as individual, vacuumed entities — that they refer to as "experiences." "I'm going for the experience." "I'm so glad I had that experience." "That was a great experience." "It will be an experience." The people who talk about their "experiences" — commenting on how great they were or how glad they've had them — are never Living Legends.

Someone might ask you: "How was your college experience?" We all know that the experience he's referring to isn't the classes. It's not the learning or the intellectual (and physical too, hopefully) growth. These people are talking about *the* experience. You know, the debauchery and the drinking and the late night gatherings —

maybe the 5 a.m. lay if you were lucky. The experience they ask about isn't the one related to self-growth — but instead the very activities that detract from it.

You always hear college students specifically talking about their study abroad programs as "great experiences." It's hard to deny that an artificial (and unnecessary) gap in the middle of a college education curtails the progress and momentum that a student had been cultivating up until that point. Four months in an environment without worthwhile stimulation (the "stimulation" on study abroad programs is usually substance-induced) doesn't just stunt a young person's growth, it also causes him or her to face extreme difficulty re-integrating back into the normal (productive) college routine upon return.

Let's take a step back and ask ourselves: was that a great experience when you went to China, ate fried rice and egg rolls every day, and returned to America morbidly obese? What about the great experience of studying abroad in Australia, smoking Marlboro Reds all day on the beach with your buddies and becoming a chain smoker for the rest of your life? Or that semester experience in Berlin, where you snorted cocaine all day and night, popped "E" and had sex in nightclub bathroom stalls? You're not fooling anyone and you're not fooling yourself — nobody gets closer to Legendary status on a study abroad program.

Sometimes the "experience" happens after the college years, a scenario that is even more alarming. "I just graduated and I'm going backpacking around Asia. It's going to be a great experience."

What this guy is really saying is that he has no direction, and has consequently resolved to mindlessly wander, not to mention waste his money, time, energy, and youth on something that won't get him anywhere closer to becoming a Living Legend. Hell, he might even go missing along the way — an outcome not altogether unfortunate.

When Leonardo da Vinci painted the Mona Lisa, do you think he was telling those around him he wanted the experience of painting the Mona Lisa? Or what about when he finished, was he saying, "Painting the Mona Lisa, that was a great experience?"

What about Michael Jordan — do you think he was sitting back as a twenty-something saying, "I want to have the experience of being the best basketball player of all time?" Or now — is he going around saying, "Yeah, becoming the greatest basketball player in history. That was some great experience?"

These Living Legends weren't talking about an "experience" because their *lives* were the experience. Their long-term streams of consciousness were the experiences to end all experiences. Every moment for a Leonardo da Vinci or a Michael Jordan was invested in creating the experience *of* a life, not *in* a life.

The former contributes value to society, the latter is a misguided undertaking rooted in selfish (and usually, hedonistic) motives.

< Messages   **Maxi**   Contact

How's the business trip going? U in the hotel yet?

Yes. Just got in my second run.

Every treadmill was taken!

I had to wait 45 min

it was worth it.

What u doing now?

Relaxing now. I have white wine and Harry Potter.

Could life be any better?

Love life :-).

lol but do you?

what do you mean?

Do u really love life?

White wine and harry potter. Why aren't you working on a book right now

???

Life is about enjoying yourself sometimes.

There's no excuse for enjoyment.

What?!!

Yes there is.

Life's about being happy and appreciating what you have. Not the way you're living.

Being miserable isn't "Legendary"

If you're appreciating, you're depreciating

Omg!!!

You really are determined to not be happy.

What happened in your childhood?

I made a conscious choice to become a Legend.

Not go around half-dazed telling the world I'm "happy"

SIX

Cardboardmag.com/Legendary_Imitators

The Living Legendary blog has continued to gain huge traction, with traffic to the site nearly tripling in the last two months alone. The success has prompted the rise of a number of knock-off blogs hoping to reel in a sliver of the demographic — yet none has come even close to finding the kind of audience that Brody has amassed.

GearingupforGreatness.com teases a "lifestyle mold for unleashing the Inner Great," mimicking Brody's use of capitalization with recurring phrases like "Geared Up Great" and "Greatness Gear" — even going so far as to talk about its very own "Greatness Headquarters."

ExponentialPotential.com invites readers to "achieve *legendary* potential by *living* healthfully, actively, and productively" (italics added).

TheLegendaryErection.com, yet another copycat, claims to offer "effective methods for obtaining and sustaining a 'legendary' hard-on," recommending that visitors combine Viagra, Cialis, and low-T injections to "reach their peak." TheLegendaryErection.com — according to Roy Chadwick, its founder — claims no connection at all with Brody's site. "We give advice that runs completely counter to the nonsense of Brody's organic, holistic approach," Chadwick explains. "We provide access to real substances that can make an immediate impact on people's lives, not some mumbo-jumbo about potential and possibility." (Chadwick also informed us that sponsorship funding recently passed the $15 million mark.)

While some of these sites may appear to offer something unique, we believe they are nothing more than pale imitators of the Living Legendary brand. And thus the Legend continues... unchallenged.

Blog Post Ideas:

- Tourists: worn out and irritable for no ultimate purpose. Living Legends never "sightsee." If your purpose is to "explore the world," you aren't Living Legendary.

- Living Legends never hit the snooze button.

- People don't want to make a mess in their kitchen, but by eating out they make a mess in their body.

- Stupid nightlife discussion: which "afterparty" to go to.

- "YOLO" and how it's only applied to partying and "going crazy." Legends understand the idea of "YOLO," but use it to target efforts during the day.

- Living Legends get blackout drunk from two drinks because of low tolerance (is this too extreme? people may not relate)

- Office workers look forward to peeing because a trip to the bathroom momentarily disconnects them from the 9-hour stream of unbearable boredom. ("Replacing one stream with another....") They also seem to take pride — middle-aged men, especially — in the fact that their biological functions still work. Living Legends never look forward to bathroom trips.

- Difference between "sculpting" your body and building a body that is truly fit. Legends pursue the latter.

- Girl in public library: "People don't realize you don't have to chug it before you flip it." Said it like she was fucking Einstein.

- If you're worried about your astrological sign, you aren't Living Legendary.

- Three routes to birth control...pills, condoms, anal. Legends choose anal. (Note: look into trademarking tagline, "Legends choose anal.")

From: Trucker Sachs
To: Jon Brody
Subject: Material with Comments

Jon,

Just got through the material. See my attached comments, but in general you should rethink where you're heading with this, man. No young person will want to listen to this crap, and so this book is already dead if that's your target demographic. It's normal for kids to want to go out, socialize, and meet members of the opposite sex. To advise against this would be to counter all of what it means to be young. Plus, you sound like an overbearing parent. That's the last voice a college freshman, fresh out of the home, wants to hear.

Trucker

The Living Legendary Framework, Manuscript Chapter 5: The Legendary Mental Approach Trucker Sachs' Edits Included

Why Partiers Aren't Legends

Living Legends, by virtue of who they are and how they are wired, avoid nightlife, drinking, and partying. This may come as a shock, especially given the mainstream media's glorification of these endeavors (their positive portrayal

 TRUCKER

Then NOBODY is gonna want to be a living legend, man.

There's a reason for this bro. It's called living…LIFE. THAT'S what people want.

🔲 TRUCKER

Who is "Don Draper-esque?" Last girl I was banging had a hyphenated name — what a fucking pain.

It's pretty much always the bathtub for me. With the water running, usually.

It's got "value" if you want pussy, man.

It's not high if you know the right people. Or if you're famous. I'm famous AND connected — so I don't pay anything. I could if I had to, though. I'm rich, by the way.

That's EXACTLY WHY you go to the VIP.

Think you've got the wrong word here…

How can you make it rain if you're bankrupt? Am I missing something?

YOU lecturing on social acceptance? That's a joke.

Not lost, just drunk. Well maybe lost, but BECAUSE they're drunk.

That's why you pay CASH. AKA "make it rain," which you already covered, I think.

of club-goers, bottle-poppers, frat boy beer-pongers, and Don Draper-esque executives on the prowl). Living Legends aren't sold on such nonsense because they understand the value of their time, health, and good feelings (i.e. not waking up hung over on the living room rug).

Legends know that VIP table service in the club has little value (the only "value," ironically, is the high price tag attached) — and therefore seek an alternate (worthwhile) route towards self-fulfillment. Part of being a Legend means overcoming the herd and following an independent path — one uncorrupted by agenda-ridden manipulations.

The media tags legends as the fools buying a round at the local watering hole, or the (secretly bankrupt) folks "making it rain" at 2am in the Meatpacking District. Emptying out their wallets for a fleeting moment of social acceptance or the false notion of grandeur, these lost souls have failed to comprehend that the path to Legendary doesn't involve mounting credit card debt or multiple hours spent smiling, nodding, and awkwardly fist-pumping to ear-piercing, deafening (literally) noise levels. Nor does the path include being the social misfit doing a keg stand in the fraternity basement (later taken to the ER for stomach pumping) or the sex-starved, corpulent suit ordering an overpriced red wine at a local restaurant, trying to convince the young lady across from him that sex appeal transcends the physical organism.

The greatness of Living Legends is enduring — and arriving at Legendary status takes time. It takes effort and discipline. It takes the self-confidence to pursue an unconventional lifestyle, one that doesn't align with the standard notions of success or validation (and make no mistake: pulling up to the club in a Ferrari and dropping several "g's" on table service is no indicator of success — at least not Legendary success).

TRUCKER

This actually comes pretty natural to me.

Dude — what's a party without loud music? Also, I'm not deaf so not sure what you mean here.

Pretty sure the "misfit" here isn't the guy doing the keg stand.

I'm thinking about it now: I bet you've NEVER done a keg stand. WOW.

All that means is that the guy was a softie.

Never Trucker. I'm getting pussy left and right.

I never take girls out to dinner hoping for a lay. I find them blacked out at 2am when it's guaranteed.

If you've got the bills, you're gonna get the thrills. That's how it works.

Who wants to take time when you can be drunk in 20 minutes?

Do you mean "living legendary" here? That doesn't take "confidence," just some serious psychological trauma. You must have had a fucked up childhood, man.

Come on, dude — have you ever driven a Ferrari? You don't know what you're missing. And that's the whole problem with everything you're writing here — you write like you're an expert but you're just a buzzkill. You wouldn't know fun even if a pack of drunk co-eds fell into your bed.

TRUCKER

I'm conquering every night. Nothing "momentary" 'bout that!

Brody, I bet you're a seconds-long champion in the bedroom.

I don't think this is a real word, man.

Grey Goose is 2006. Get with it.

I usually need 7.

MULTIPLE stacks is ideal.

What about a group of bitches that you wanna bang? I've done that MANY times and it works like a charm.

I'm snorting lines behind the velvet rope, and I AM famous.

It's MDMA now, so you know.

The way I party IS hard work.

I'm usually tuned into ESPN. But if I get back from the bar really late without a chick (which is rare, btw), I do like the Showtime late hour.

I think you mean "image."

Nobody is "thinking" when they're seven deep.

No young person reading this is gonna wanna think about math, bro.

You were young once, grandpa?

Living Legendary isn't about becoming a momentary conqueror, or a seconds-long champion experiencing fleeting recognition, ephemeral machismo, and a non-enduring sense of importance. It's not about ordering a fancy wine or a bottle of Grey Goose topped with a firecracker. Nor is it about downing four Red Bulls so you can stay up past four in the morning. Legendary status doesn't come from flashing a stack of hundreds to a group of strangers, or closing yourself off behind a velvet rope and two 300-pound ex-convicts so you can snort lines while feeling famous. Indeed, Legends are separated and elevated from the masses... by their character, not the velvet rope. They are unique in a real, lasting way — one that comes from investing years of hard work and energy into the right channels.

Yet it seems as though people take part in this mirage of "partying" — strive for it, even — without second thought, almost like it's a granted part of the equation. When I was an adolescent, an older "role model" then in college gave me what he called "golden advice," advice I would "certainly thank [him] for one day." "You have to drink a glass of water after a long night out before going to sleep," he explained with a look that indicated he had just given me the key to life. "If you drink some water right before bed, you won't feel so miserable the next day." Never in this role model's imagination could he fathom a scenario where this advice simply wouldn't be applicable to my life. It was standard protocol, relevant and useful to all. What if I wasn't going to be having long nights out, or any nights out at all? What if I didn't plan to spend the next day miserable? What if I was going to be fast asleep at the hour of the water glass — which I'm guessing in his mind was around four in the morning?

Similarly, I was in the lobby of my South Florida apartment building when I overheard the doorman asking an obese young lady (and fellow resident) about her college experience. "Are you keeping it under control?" Is going out of control — meaning going out drinking every night,

 TRUCKER

That's good advice actually. I would do it more often if I weren't so plastered every time I got home.

You could use a few more. Seems like you're not even living at all, actually. You're quarantined or some shit.

I think your life is beyond anyone's imagination, man.

Yea, it's because you're not living.

Then you're a loser.

All good things involve suffering. That's actually a motto you should be familiar with.

With the way you're living, you might as well be in a PERMANENT sleep.

Six or seven would be more accurate.

Wait. You're telling me YOU LIVE IN SOUTH FLORIDA AND DON'T GO OUT?? What kind of freak are you?

You're not published and you have a doorman?

Yes.

TRUCKER

Yes.

Not sure about this one. I don't bang fat chicks. Or at least try not to. Sometimes I'm just totally gone and it happens.

I'm not, man. The bitches love my bod.

So are you saying no steak before drinks? Cuz that's usually how I start off my big nights.

Ok man. This is way too extreme.

of course — simply a staple component of the college years? And if you're not drinking — in essence, "keeping it under control," as the doorman put it — are you failing to live your life to the fullest? What if you're so fat you can't even transport yourself from one bar to the next? If you're obese, your body is already trashed, before you get "trashed" in the traditional sense. Pouring alcohol on top will only add to the "pile." The result? A walking landfill.

Ok just meet there. It should be fine.

5:45 PM

Dude are you alright??

Yea. Luckily nothing is broken.

That guy came out of nowhere

I had no idea about all of this! We could have gone somewhere else.

U should have told me.

Trust me if I thought THAT was gonna happen I would have.

I'm at home icing the arm and neck now.

I think I'll be fine

That's good. I hope you feel better

From: Donna Livingston
To: Jon Brody
Subject: RE: Query

Dear Jon, Thank you very much for sending along your proposal
and the link to your blog which I looked over for quite a bit of time.
You definitely make a great fitness and health guru for the young
generation. The issue with the book however, as I see it, is that your
background and credentials are too thin right now. You are putting
yourself in the position as the expert with very few credentials
and readers and publishers will want to know — who is your
expert nutritionist, athletic trainer, mentor, and what are your own
accomplishments that give you the authority to propose this plan?

Your plan is quite out there, but more or less it makes sense to me —
and it's appealing that it's being delivered from a young, fresh up-
and-coming athletic star. That's all good but in my opinion there has
to be much more heft and meat and potatoes to a book if your goal
is for a publisher to buy it. When it comes to lifestyle/health/fitness
books, you are competing with media gurus and big players so I would
recommend that you build more of a business and following, get
interviews with top experts in the industry who will support your plan
and really build your blog and media following, twitter, etc. It seems as
though you have a little franchise — and that's fantastic — but what's
beneath the cover is too thin. If you have an endorsement deal with a
big corporation like Nike or Whole Foods, for instance, and you become
their spokesperson or a spokesman for another company — that will
put you in a better position to get published, too. Again, thank you so
much for your considering me and please stay in touch if your business
expands and the book develops more in depth.

Good luck! Best regards, Donna

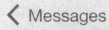

Messages **Alex** Contact

> Hey man. Didn't get a chance to tell you the other day with all the commotion, but you're really not looking healthy.

> Fuck this job it's killing you.

> Take some time off to lose weight.

I need to make money.

One more year maybe I can figure out something else.

> you might be dead by then

I'll be fine.

Real people need real jobs.

> True. But I'm still worried about you.

> Look if you were making millions I would maybe say do it. But this just isn't worth it.

> I think you should worry a little more about yourself.

> I don't think "healthy" means being tackled by undercover cops at Whole Foods checkout aisles.

LivingLegendaryBlog.com

Avoid the Microwave

There are two reasons Living Legends don't use the microwave. (1) Microwaves degrade the nutritional quality of your food. (2) Microwaves cause cancer — both from the effects on the food itself, as well as from rays emitted from the machine when it's on. (Never let anyone "fry your brains out" by letting them use the microwave with you in the room.)

The best way to avoid the microwave is to purchase an industrial steamer. Some may find this excessive given how large industrial steamers are (approximately the same size as a refrigerator), but make

no mistake: this tool will prove critical in your quest to become a
Living Legend. If you live in an apartment and can't fit the steamer
inside your kitchen, there's always enough room in the bedroom.
In fact, the steamer *is* in the bedroom at the Headquarters despite
there being ample space in the cooking quarters, because Jon Brody
wants to be sure he can prepare a batch of freshly-steamed baby bok
choy or red cabbage without having to leave the room. (Brody also
maintains a mini-fridge at his bedside with a backup stash of organic
produce — just in case). Having possession of an industrial steamer
will allow you to prepare fresh organic vegetables at a moment's
notice, without heading down the fifteen-year chemotherapy track.

COMMENTS (2)

CHUCK

My grandson put me on to this blog. I want to comment that I've
been using microwaves for over forty years and am healthy (no
cancer). This isn't true. I don't know anybody who owns an "industrial
steamer." Come to think of it, I've never actually seen one. Do these
really exist?

JON BRODY

They do exist. And so does your cancer.
You just don't know it yet.

TWEETS	FOLLOWING	FOLLOWERS	FAVORITES	LISTS
425	5K	80K	1,012	3

Tweets   Tweets & replies   Photos & videos

Living Legendary @LvngLgndry · 5h
The protocol of your life should never be 1) get drunk 2) see what happens
#sobersex #drinkingsucks #livinglegendary

↩ 0   ↻ 2   ★ 1

Cardboardmag.com/Living_Legendary_Leak

Cardboard Mag's investigative unit obtained a leaked email this week, sent from Jon Brody to The Fresh Market, Inc. — the high-end grocery chain — in which the Living Legendary founder proposes a partnership with the company. In addition to shedding further light on Brody's delusional aspirations (who would want this maniac at the helm of their brand?), the note also revealed that Brody has recently been barred from all Whole Foods Markets nationally after he failed to settle payment on a bag of rice. Brody writes:

"Whole Foods has made it crystal clear that they do not want to associate with the Living Legendary brand. It is because of this that I write to you, their primary competitor, asking if you would like to embrace me as an ambassador and spokesman."

Herbert Lang, head of public relations for The Fresh Market, declined an interview with Cardboard Mag on the grounds that the story wasn't "natural," but we have it on good authority that all Brody's request will lead to is a restraining order.

The Living Legendary Framework, Manuscript Chapter 5: The Legendary Mental Approach

"Going Out": Explained

What is the meaning behind this phrase "going out?" We all "go out" all the time don't we? To the park, the supermarket, or the gym — maybe to pay a visit to Aunt Jane every now and again. But there's a distinct meaning to the expression, "I'm going out," which can be translated as: "I'm a horny little piece of shit who's tired of not getting laid, who's afraid to approach women in daily life, and who has to dumb himself down to have the slight *possibility* — still not guaranteed — of relieving his sexual urges (in some way than alone in front of a computer screen)."

While this gender-specific "translation" delivers a hit to the male night-lifer, you really can't blame him for taking part in the whole thing. After all, this jungle-like environment is conducive to a man's natural inclinations to have sex with multiple women — potentially several in the same night if he slips a twenty or two to the washroom attendant. But a perceptive individual (and ideally, future Living Legend) will quickly realize the nightlife scene is more illusion than anything. While it appears as though there are countless appealing options for "getting lucky" — swarms of girls dressed in short dresses and revealing tops — most of these women are either "just looking to just have fun" in the sense of dressing up and socializing with girlfriends (if that's your intention, why didn't you just go for an early dinner?), out with their boyfriend, seemingly appealing from a distance but alarmingly unattractive and worn when you actually get up close for a conversation, "turning tricks" — which, if you're already coughing up dough for $15 cocktails, you likely won't have reserves to afford, just not interested in talking to you (because they're not drunk enough, you're out of shape, or both), or planted there and paid an hourly wage by the bar manager to sell more drinks. Whichever way you look at it, a woman who is actually looking for sex in the context of a 2 a.m. club or bar scene is very much suspect. Sure, maybe they're horny — but any girl who's grown up on Disney movies ought to know: Prince Charming never pops up out of a Little West 12th Street watering hole.

One tip to always remember: going out to a bar horny is like going out to a restaurant hungry. You'll never feel satiated because the product you're getting — while it may be presented nicely and taste good while you're eating it — is always void in quality and lacking the proper nutrition.

It is important to note briefly here that Legends never live for the pursuit of sex. They live to become Living Legends. A large percentage of people define their lives by their love lives — who they're sleeping with or who they're trying to sleep with. Living Legends understand that it's their daily routines that should be the main focus — the constant struggle towards Legendary — *not* an all-night pursuit of a lay. Of course, Legends enjoy a healthy love life on the side — but they never lose perspective.

 Notes

Interesting quote from Perfect Curves Magazine for possible use:

- "Women around the world are taking ownership of their bodies by fighting back against outdated conceptions about what it means to be beautiful, specifically those that put pressure on women with a curvier body structure. This past summer, thousands of women joined hand-in-hand to participate in a 'Fatkini' swimsuit photoshoot, which was later featured in an online spread that was shared by millions. It was a strong statement that these women could be beautiful without the pressure of slimming down. And in a controversial hit track from Beyonce that upped female self-identity to a delightful new level, having a 'big, fat behind' was praised as the new ideal for female beauty."

From: Jon Brody
To: Rogaine, Inc.
Subject: Rogaine Spokesman
Attn: Hank Harriman, Chief Marketing Officer

Dear Mr. Harriman,

My name is Jon Brody and I am an Ivy League graduate with a lifestyle franchise in the making — "Living Legendary." I am writing because I am a Rogaine user (have been for the past five years, since the age of nineteen), entrepreneur, innovator, author, and health/fitness guru looking to partner with a company as their spokesman. I believe I could be a good candidate to represent your brand, specifically in assisting

Rogaine reach the 16–24-year-old demographic, which would be a smart investment given the average onset of hair loss is much younger now (due to, as I'm sure you're aware, the modern food landscape: added hormones in animal products, artificial additives in processed foods, genetically-modified ingredients, pesticide-ridden produce, etc.) I've included a link to my blog and three chapters of my book, which I hope you will glance at when time permits. I look forward to hearing from you and hope we can work together. Best regards, Jon Brody

From: Hank Harriman
To: Jon Brody
Subject: RE: Rogaine Spokesman

Dear Jon,

After an extensive review of your blog and background, we would be delighted to take you on as a spokesman. We will be in touch by phone this week.

Best, Hank Harriman

SEVEN

Just got home. The entire counter is STAINED BLOOD RED!

Did you cook beets again?

Yes, ma. Early this morning

How many times do I have to tell you to USE A CUTTING BOARD?????

I was in a rush.

Racing out the door for my workout.

Start looking for your own place.

And a job. I won't be paying your rent

The Living Legendary Framework, Manuscript Chapter 2: Building the Legendary Body

The Legend of Smiling Feet

The Legendary body can only be built — and maintained — through regular massage. Because Legends pursue a strenuous fitness routine, they require deep tissue massages *three to four times per week* (for at least one hour per session). This is the only way Legends can recover fully from workouts and stay healthy in the long run.

Legends understand the importance of finding foreign therapists, as it's well-understood that American masseurs are generally entitled, lacking in skill, uncompromising due to a delusional confidence in their knowledge, and completely unwilling to exert themselves to full capacity or accommodate the customer with what he or she wants.

Fortunately (and not by chance), there is a Chinese-run reflexology massage parlor — "Smiling Feet" — located five minutes from the Living Legendary Headquarters. Smiling Feet provides a one-of-a-kind massage setting: a single communal room filled with reclining massage chairs, in which Smiling Feet clients can enjoy their services in one another's company. Legends can always count on Smiling Feet's therapists (all Chinese and all armed with only two English words: "relax" and "tip") to provide a deep, thorough rubdown, for a price you can't beat ($25/hour). And the therapists will do whatever you ask (while smiling, too).

Yet the Smiling Feet bargain does come with a price — as the experience is anything but glamorous. Smiling Feet won't transport you to some other worldly place of inner peace and relaxation. It's all about utility. *Utility without one ounce of relaxation.* The Smiling Feet soundtrack, aside from the same three Enya songs on repeat, includes fellow patrons snoring or talking on their phones, employees hocking up loogies at the "front desk" (a folding card table), and employees aggressively opening and closing the microwave door in their makeshift "lounge."

The sights and smells are obstacles for a Legend to overcome. Entering the bathroom unannounced (a broken lock has rendered it a hidden door) might provide a short glimpse into the private life of a Smiling Feet therapist.

And, it's standard protocol for a Smiling Feet therapist not to wash his hands between clients — and part of your responsibility as a patron, assuming you want to avoid contracting ringworm or impetigo, is to remind him.

But these are all features, not flaws. Smiling Feet is made for Legend-building not just because of the quality massage but the mental adversity that must be overcome. As you will learn in the chapters to come, it's only by overcoming this type of adversity that an aspiring Legend can arrive at his final destination.

LivingLegendaryBlog.com

You Can't Outwork a Bad Diet

There was a small poster tacked onto the wall somewhere in the
Ivy League collegiate strength and conditioning center that read, "You
can't outwork a bad diet." This saying is right on point. Even if an
individual lives a healthy and active lifestyle, with a poor diet, he will
never be able to "outwork" the contamination present within his body.

Exercising *while* on a bad diet actually exacerbates the potency of the unhealthy food. Just like trying to contain the venom of a snake bite by tying a piece of string around the affected area, if you refrain from exercise while eating poorly, the poison is contained within the digestive track. As soon as you exercise with unhealthy food in your system, the increased circulation of the body serves to spread this "venom" throughout the organism. Once the heart starts pumping with vigor, the contaminants are propelled to every extremity and every organ. The cancer-causing agents of processed foods, the pesticides of non-organic vegetables, and the hormones of farm-raised meats are all released and carried throughout.

Living Legends work out and eat healthy food. It's not an either/or. It's both.

> Lean??! You told me you would take care of him!

> He looks like he's about to die.

> He'll be fine. He's feeling better than ever.

> He can hardly walk two feet without collapsing!!

> OMG you are so IRRESPONSIBLE.

> You're going to have to find a new living arrangement. I don't want you in my house anymore.

The Living Legendary Framework, Manuscript Chapter 14: Finding Passion

Short-Term Self-Interest vs. Long-Run Contribution

My cousin Mia is thirty-two years old, and has spent her entire life in Philadelphia. During her high school years, she had difficulty finding a core group of friends and struggled to fit in. In college, majoring in history and pursuing a handful of classes in the visual arts, Mia never came to identify a true passion. Her father helped to secure a job for her at a financial services firm upon graduation, and she has stayed there ever since. Mia goes to work every day, takes care of her bills and other responsibilities, meets friends for dinner several evenings per week, and has fostered relationships with several long-term boyfriends — all the while suffering from a severe psychological affliction.

The manifestation of her problem is not obvious, for she functions fine on a daily basis. Her work superiors laud her for a strong work ethic. Her friends attest she is energized and upbeat. Mia's college interest in history has prompted her to join a local "MeetUp" group, where she reads and discusses biographies of historical figures. Yet every time I interact with Mia, the effects of her issue — "untempered selflessness," as I like to call it — are glaringly apparent.

"Untempered selflessness" is a condition that arises from a series of inter-related conditions — anxiety, psychological trauma, excessive shyness, social phobia — and results in a person accommodating others unnecessarily, to such an extreme that it takes a toll on his or her own wellbeing. In her job, Mia takes on an unmanageable workload because she can't say no to her colleagues — resulting in late nights up working. Whenever she watches an infomercial advertising a charity, she sends a check. If it's raining late at night and there's a shortage of taxis, Mia will shrink from the curb if she notices anyone else on her corner trying to hail one, even if this means getting wet. Mia's sister finds it sad that Mia is "so nice, that if [she] and a stranger were the last two people on the earth, and there was one piece of bread left, she would unhesitatingly give it to the stranger."

In her daily routines, Mia is so focused on the needs of others that she becomes overwhelmed, flustered, and forgetful. In her quest to secure that everyone around her is comfortable and content, she loses track of her own stream of consciousness. As a result, she has been the cause of several small fires in her apartment building after leaving appliances on. Mia sets alarms for the birthdays of friends and family members months in advance, yet once she turns off the reminders and goes about her day, she forgets about it. Realizing this days later, Mia sends a distressed apology so long-winded you would have thought she missed her own wedding.

Mia's flustered state has created severe anxiety, which in turn has triggered the adult expression of a dormant gene for Tourette's syndrome. Over the past seven years, Mia has developed a twitch where she unexpectedly jerks her head straight back, as if someone dealt her a forceful upper-cut. This has not only caused embarrassment for Mia, but physical harm to those around her. While out to dinner with the family at a fancy restaurant, Mia's head suddenly flipped back into the crotch of a Tuxedoed waiter, launching the scalding tea-water he was carrying backwards and onto the shoulders of several patrons at the adjacent table, causing third-degree burns.

Mia's problem is the product of a misallocation of her personal resources — time, money, and health. She is doing the opposite of Living Legendary. In many ways, Mia's over-the-top concern about others stems from her own failure to identify an *internal* direction, one aligned with a unique passion or interest. While Living Legends do influence the world positively, their everyday pursuits are targeted investments *in themselves*. Sure, give a few coins to a beggar if the impulse arises, but then invest the rest of your funds into *yourself* so you can arrive at Legendary status. After all, it's very likely your final contribution can end up bringing thousands of beggars off the streets in the process.

From: Michael Brody
To: Jon Brody
Subject: Privacy

Jon, Just got through Chapter 14 and the Mia (a.k.a. Jessica) story needs to be deleted. All the stories need to be deleted — and I need an assurance in writing that you will see to this. You need to remember that if you do get a book deal, the publisher will be worried that your content could provoke third party cause of action related to invasion of privacy or defamation. You and the publisher will have to think about possible liabilities with your stories and references.

I want to be direct here by saying that the Brody's want to keep their privacy. There will be no direct references to the Brody's since the details are all private and your stories are factually incorrect. We want our privacy not to be compromised in your current book or any future books, blogs, public appearances, media communications, etc. If this story about Cousin Jessica were to get out — or any of the anecdotes about Uncle Harry or Cousin Lisa — there would be significant negative consequences for them, both from an emotional standpoint and in their professional lives. I am confident you wouldn't want to harm Jessica or anyone else.

There is no need to talk about your book further, but I will need to look over any parts that might in any way pertain to my family or me. You will also have to send me a draft prior to publication so that I may review the contents.   Please assure me in writing that you agree to all of this.

Your Dad

Smiling Feet

12 reviews

$ · Massage Parlors

Legendary Critic

Smiling Feet is a great destination for aspiring Legends because the staff present clients with challenging mental and physical obstacles. If you can overcome a Smiling Feet massage without lasting psychological trauma, it means you're on your way to Legendary. A few tips for a manageable experience: (1) if a sudden thunderous, machine gun-esque rattling overcomes your section of the massage room, ask the owner to adjust the ceiling panels adjacent to the AC duct with his broomstick (you shouldn't have to pay a supplementary fee for him to do this); (2) ask for "Clean Nails," an alias among returning patrons for the therapist Kevin, who is known to have the best hygiene of the twenty-one and half person staff (Tito — the final half of the employment tallee —

I wouldn't recommend because at 3' 5", his go-to massage technique is a form of rolfing where he somersaults on top of unsuspecting, downward-facing customers); (3) when you're not seated in a massage chair or lying on a massage table, keep your footwear on at all times — the location's name can be a bit misleading in the sense that a single "unprotected" step on the Smiling Feet floor will infect you with a form of athlete's foot so severe that no treatment stands a chance at remedy.

The Living Legendary Framework, Manuscript Chapter 5: The Legendary Mental Approach

Nightlife: A Legend-Killing Cycle

Pursuers of night life are full-blown addicts, completely dependent on the lifestyle, their fellow indulgers, and the substances that fuel them. Their routine usually involves a long week of suffering at a bland office job, waiting for the arrival of the weekend — where they will purge their pent-up frustration, only to begin the cycle again the following week. A gradual decline in health brings the unsuspecting victim closer and closer to death.

The 1980s rock band "Loverboy" — in their mega-hit "Working for the Weekend" — pinpoints the essence of the phenomenon. "Everyone's wondering will you come out tonight… everybody's working for the weekend… everybody's going off the deep end…" The "weekend" for Loverboy is synonymous with nightlife. And things have only gotten worse since the song was released in 1981.

The social interaction in nightlife is superficial — brief eye-contact and a nod, a cordial smile, a four-word exchange between bass vibrations, a handshake, or pat on the back. True friendships and relationships are never crafted in the bowels of nightlife — only short-lived banter with a familiar face, or a second hook-up with a former one-night stand. Yet nightlifers crave it all. Why? (1) They don't want to head down a destructive path alone; (2) waving to familiar faces inside a crowded venue contributes to a (non-existent, of course) sense of status; and (3) seeing the same people out validates the pursuit by making it seem sensible. "If these other people keep coming back, there has to be *something* constructive about it," a thirty-year-old lawyer might "reason."

The symbol most destructive is the cup, glass, or bottle that is ever-affixed to a nightlifer's hand. Like robots running on an electric charge, partiers simply cannot function without their life-juice an arm-raise away. The "Path of the Cup" (as Legends refer to it) is an instrumental part of life for the non-Legends among us, and it doesn't end once the evening is over, for when dawn arrives, a new cup — the coffee cup — replaces the wine or beer from the previous night. It's a neverending cycle that erodes one's natural biological processes, energy levels, good-feelings, health, and sober state *in going about life* — to the point of no reversal.

Exiting the local community college library the other day, I overheard a student explaining his plan for the following afternoon — when he would have completed his last final exam, and along with it, the semester. "I just want to sit down and drink. No wining or dining. No going out. Just sit and drink." A heavily-shared Facebook status reads: "It's amazing how our attitude changes towards alcohol: as a teenager you go, 'I don't like the taste of it but I wanna look cool,' then in your twenties you're like, 'You know what? This gives me the confidence to talk to the opposite sex,' and then in your forties you're like, "You know what? This is the only thing I like about being alive.'"

If you don't like the taste of something, it probably means it's bad for you. And if you need a stimulant to talk to a girl, then you're not the man you ought to be. Toil towards Legendary and gain some confidence — instead of dumbing yourself down to the point you forgot you didn't have any. Lastly, if drinking is the only thing you like about being alive, then you've failed, completely and absolutely.

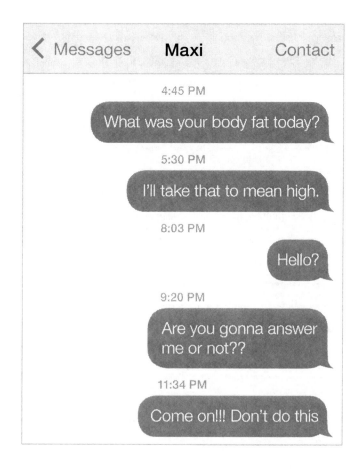

From: Jon Brody
To: Jon Brody
Subject: Once Dark, Do NOT Leave House

You just woke up and it's not even light out yet. You're jumping out of your skin! Face bloated and fingers completely swollen. Your sleep cycle totally disrupted. Remember this. Remember how you're feeling. DO NOT EVER DRINK AGAIN!!!!!!
Why isn't Maxi responding?? What a bitch.
Doesn't matter though. You need to stick with your routine. If this book gets taken and they find you out at night in a bar you'll be the laughing stock. Totally going against everything you preach. Print this out today and stick it above your bed: " One drink, once per year."

LivingLegendaryBlog.com

A Boob Job Can Save a Life

Sometimes Legends must pursue unconventional measures to get where they need. It's an unfortunate reality for aspiring female Legends that their ultimate fate is heavily dependent on their physical appearance (more so than for men). There's a saying Living Legends adhere to behind closed doors: "A boob job can save a life." It can mean the difference between securing an eligible boyfriend or not. Getting that job promotion or hitting a glass ceiling. Enjoying a happy family life or fading into the abyss of singledom. In an ideal world, Legends would only need to invest in the body through substantive channels. But it's always useful to remember: if circumstances are dire, a couple of D-cups certainly won't hurt.

COMMENTS (2)

SALLY

This is not only offensive, it's sexist. And not true.

CRAZY

You're out of your mind buddy.

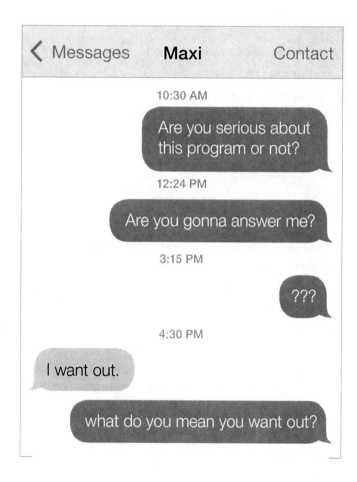

of the workout program

then I want out of the relationship

Ok fine!!!

You're crazy

I'm going to start dating teenagers. Before the American food has had time to fatten them.

you do that. call me from jail.

EIGHT

Jon Brody, 26

less than a mile away   Last Active 26 minutes ago

If you've got heft, swipe left.

I'm a blogger, author, and Ivy League graduate with the body of an Olympic athlete looking for a lean, toned, educated woman to match.

No back fat, cankles, or cellulite. No lower back, nipple, arm, toe, finger, or butt hair.

Must have straight teeth and work out twice per day, with at least one hour free every night to read drafts of writing. Must be willing to eat chard stalks, radish leaves, carrot hairs, beet skin, and strawberry tops.

Height/weight specifications: 5' 5" and under 100lbs. Each additional inch means you may add (but ideally, you won't have to) an additional 4 lbs. Shoe size women's 7 or below (already know to specify women's sizes, from past experiences haha ;-)) .

Not looking for "love." Utilitarian-based relationship. Intimacy 4x per week and sleep in separate rooms. There is a twin mattress in my walk-in closet if you're inclined to stay over.

No movie or restaurant night. All "dates" will take place inside the apartment in order to optimally control food quality and portion sizes.

Notice*: Before meeting, two full-length body shots (front and profile) must be provided (FILTER FREE), along with an annotated list of any periods at which weight exceeded 150 lbs (include years, length of time, and reason for). Upon meeting, a full body inspection will be conducted (including the use of a body fat percentage clamp) before any conversation takes place.

Sarah, 22

35 miles away   Last Active 5 hours ago

?

How much do you weigh?

 Ummm...why?

Cuz I think we have a lot in common. Wanted to see if it would be worth the time to meet up...

5:45 PM

How often do you work out?

Automatic Reply: Sarah has blocked you from her match list.

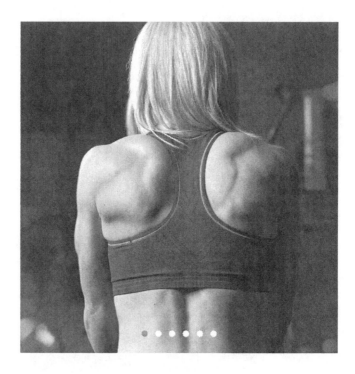

Nicke, 27

15 miles away   Last Active 5 hours ago

I'm tranny.

Nicke

10:00 AM

What are you training for? ;-)

2:37 PM

Sometimes I'm so tired from workouts I mispell too haha ;-)! That's between me and you though ;-) ..I'm a writer so I can't admit these things publicly lol

 I'm tranny.

Triathlete? Great! I played sports in college. In the Ivy League ;-)

The Living Legendary Framework, Manuscript Chapter 9: Legendary Romance

Take a Closer Look

When it comes to romance, taking a closer look can save a Legend much in the way of future hassle. During my early college years — my philosophies not yet fully formed — I would often go out to bars with male friends, in pursuit of girls. For some reason, it always seemed I was dealt the worst-looking one of the bunch, who also happened to be the horniest (and more often than not, a drug addict). Having wasted away the night with my crew (and the third-wheel reject passed along to me), I often would decide to head home alone while my friends went back to their dorm rooms with their new conquests.

Experiences like these converted me into a careful observer of the world of romance and the tricks of the trade. One girl I got roped into dating for several weeks was mysteriously obese from the waist down — but was initially able to conceal her leg girth through the "black-tights illusion." It took me five dates to get her back to the apartment, and when the pants eventually came off, I nearly passed out. Another girl made me believe she had perfectly straight hair, spending hours prepping herself before each date and avoiding the ocean or pool all summer (explaining that the summer months were prime for sea lice infestation). It was only until I flirtatiously pushed her into the playground sprinklers during a walk in the park that her hair took natural form: curlier than the Third Stooge. Yet another acquaintance sported a massive sore on her lower lip — one that never quite seemed to heal. I asked her if it was herpes and she denied it. I snapped some photos of the bugger while she was sleeping and my dermatologist confirmed my worst fear.

Take a closer look when it comes to the background of a romantic partner. A former girlfriend — Sandra — had a perfect nose. It was otherworldly, like it had walked straight off some spaceship from the land of the flawless. Strange thing was, when you looked at the family, not one of them had a nose anything like it. Moreover, Sandra had no photos on Facebook or around her house before age nineteen — almost as if that was when she had landed on Earth. It was only when I found myself digging through some old shoeboxes in Sandra's attic (when she and her family were out and the house was empty) that I uncovered the early teenage photos I needed to confirm my suspicions.

Take a closer look at the possibility your partner may be hoping for an "accidental" pregnancy. Young, unmarried women with small children have become ubiquitous here in Florida and elsewhere. With all of the modern contraceptive measures out there, an unintended pregnancy in the modern era is suspect. The last thing an aspiring Legend needs is a casual-fling-turned-fatherhood-turned-marriage.

Take a closer look when it comes to lovers of cats, dogs, and all things furry. Lovers of furry things are often strategically working to build this image. It's a calculated move to make you believe they are innocent, harmless, benevolent creatures — when in fact, they are connivers. These people have well-planned, expertly-executed agendas to get you to marry them and they will pursue their goal mercilessly — even if that means running over a few stray cats along the way.

Kathy, 20

30 miles away   Active 1 hour ago

Working every day to get to chick-fil-a in time
for a breakfast biscuit

That wasn't a joke

Wait so you eat chick fil a everyday?

 Yes!

I don't think it's smart to meet up. Anyway you probably won't make it more than a few months.

Make it? Chick fil a isn't closing down anytime soon haha. And I don't plan to change my morning schedule.

Make it in the sense of you continuing to live

 Lol. You're a funny guy

Let's plan on this: If your heart's still beating in six months and you're still on this thing, write me

Chloe, 21

30 miles away   Active 1 hour ago

South Florida living. Get Blonder. Get Tanner.

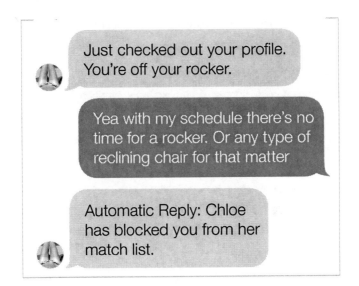

The Living Legendary Framework, Manuscript Chapter 9: Legendary Romance

Nightlife Sharking

When it comes to the pursuit of sex, a Living Legend's energies and time are fully targeted. When a Legend spends time in a bar or club (Legends will never be found in a fraternity basement, house party, or other venue of blue-collar revelry) after 10 p.m., he surely isn't intoxicated, socializing, or merely "having fun." A true Legend is geared up for one purpose only: finding and securing a suitable (and, ideally, repeat) partner for sex.

Nightlife can — and should — be enjoyed *once per week, sober, and for an hour and a half window* (ideally ending before midnight so your sleep isn't compromised) to identify and engage with prospective mates in a no-bullshit manner. Use the highly-concentrated crowd to your advantage to spot what you like, approach him or her, and make the connection. There's no time to waste during the hour and a half because the more connections you make, the easier it will be to lock down a steady partner for sexual release. It's crucial that you limit yourself to only an hour and a half because this compressed time block will force your highly-focused approach. For a Living Legend, there's no room to be shy — so get out of your shell and start meeting the people you want to.

Americans are, of course, usually fat. If your preference is to find a thin mate, it's wise to frequent nightlife settings that cater to an international audience — particularly Europeans.

It's important to note here that Living Legends never use online dating because the quality of daters is generally low, and as a result, extensive time must be invested sorting through profiles to find an acceptable match. Also, attractiveness is heavily exaggerated in online dating due to carefully-selected (and extensively-filtered) profile photos — so you will often find yourself wasting time meeting people who grossly misrepresent what they look like. Living Legends always seek romantic partners in person. If your circumstances are extreme and you're forced to use online dating, you should outsource the sorting through profiles to a third party (a $7 hourly wage is standard) so you don't waste your valuable time.

The lifestyle of a Living Legend makes sexual release less critical than it might otherwise be, thanks to the strenuous physical and mental routines that are at the core of Living Legendary.   Put simply, Legends are constantly on edge.   When you're drained, your libido will naturally be lower and so you probably won't be wanting to seek out sex in the first place.   A naturally low libido is one of the primary signifiers of Living Legendary, because it's only a true Legend that can deplete himself to the point of having zero sex drive.

Cardboardmag.com/Jon_Brody_as_Rogaine_ Spokesman

Well, what do you know — Brody found a taker.   Despite his full head of hair, Brody has convinced Rogaine, Inc. — the hair-loss topical solution brand — to take him on as their leading spokesman, where he appears in a widespread advertising campaign that targets the younger demographic.   Brody is shirtless in the new promotional materials, waxed from the waist up save for a healthy (and seemingly fuller, compared with shots from earlier blog material) mane of long black hair — pointing straight at the camera with one hand as the other hovers above his scalp with a Rogaine 1 ml measuring dropper. Various taglines complement the images: "Keeping your hair will keep you sane.   Start now with Rogaine." — playing on Jon Brody's well-known reputation as a crazy man; "Legends tackle problems before they start," part of Rogaine's new campaign to start using the product *before* you notice hair loss; and "You can't nightlife shark bald," a reference to Brody's recently-released book excerpt about picking up women at nightclubs and bars. As a result of the ad campaign, Rogaine has benefited from some well-needed buzz, with many other heavily-followed blogs posting about the partnership. Brody's association with Rogaine has helped the Living Legendary blog too, as the audience has increased exponentially over the course of the last two months, ringing in 3.5 million page views in that time.

We sat down with Hank Harriman to discuss the course of events.

CM: Who in your company came up with this baffling idea to contract Jon Brody as a spokesman?

Mr. Harriman: Well actually, Brody was the one who contacted us. It was his idea to try to market to a younger audience. We've long been looking for a way in to that demographic, and he gave us the excuse to try it.

CM: The ad campaign has benefitted Brody's Living Legendary blog perhaps even more than it has benefitted Rogaine. Does that concern you?

Harriman: We're happy for it to be a win-win situation, as long as he keeps posting about his hair.

CM: Has Brody's role as a spokesman had an effect on sales?

Harriman: We think it will. Our plan is that Jon Brody can help us make hair loss cool. Or at least make it acceptable to admit you are losing your hair. And if you're able to keep your hair, that is even cooler.

LivingLegendaryBlog.com

Stick to Your Skillset

Living Legends see their situation at face value — and never allow unbridled optimism to taint a realistic perspective. While out at a bar as a 20-year-old, I initiated a dialogue with an attractive girl — Samantha — who told me she was an aspiring model. Samantha's modeling career took off later that year when she was featured in a centerfold spread in *Hustler*, which opened doors for her to pose in other adult magazines. Recently (now five years later), I ran into her at the supermarket and she explained that nude modeling was a thing of the past for her. Samantha was now branching off into the business side of the industry — a more "refined" path, in her eyes. Apparently, her associates were looking past her fake tits to everything else she had to offer. No, not her perfect butt, long legs, or all-American smile — these suits saw other potential. They had identified a unique business acumen and strategic intuition that only a shirtless college drop-out, dildo-in-hand, could possess.

Samantha explained that she would soon be flying to Europe on a charter for a private meeting with a world-renowned businessman. The two would be discussing a new video-sharing "app" for the iPhone and its potential in international markets — for which she had put together an extensive PowerPoint presentation. Was Samantha aware of the real agenda for the meeting — and that any spread-sheets she had prepared would be secondary to her spreading *herself* on the sheets? Probably not. As a result, Samantha would enter a most uncomfortable situation once she arrived — and likely suffer for it. Living Legends can't afford this. If you want to Live Legendary, stick to your skill set and make the most of it — and never succumb to the allure of too-good-to-be-true scenarios that have little basis in reality.

From: Jon Brody
To: Customer Service, Tinder, Inc.
Subject: Match List

Hello,

I live in the South Florida area and recently downloaded the Tinder app. I've been logging in several hours per day but have yet to swipe right: all of the profiles that appear are of overweight persons. Is the app exclusively for the overweight?

Many of my (thin) friends do use the app and have had success with it, which is why I'm wondering if there might be some glitch in my software. Two days ago, I upgraded to Tinder Plus with the hopes of finding matches in nearby cities, but these locations display exclusively obese profiles too. Please let me know if there is a setting I might adjust or a feature I should unlock. Thank you. Jon Brody

The Living Legendary Framework, Manuscript Chapter 16: Sunday Brunch and Other Atrocities

<u>Sunday Brunch</u>

Somebody's gotta ask it: what the hell are people thinking when they mobilize their large, sick, tired, hung over frames for a Sunday brunch? After a long night "out on the town" — complete with an empty-calorie restaurant meal, followed by more empty-calorie cocktails — Sunday brunchers wake up bright-eyed and bushy-tailed, thoroughly disillusioned with purpose and mistakenly believing they will be adding value to the world that day by downing starch under many names (pancakes, bagels, English muffins, waffles, French toast, etc.). Continuing the self-destruction marathon that began over half a day prior, brunchers proceed to ingest more helpings of body-killing, life-shortening gruel, whose poisonous effects are further augmented by (or "paired with" — a savvy restaurant owner's ploy to make the whole tragic scene seem elegant) various cocktails.

Add the fact that these folks have been sitting in an office all week — steadily deconditioning and growing stiffer by the hour and snacking on breakfast pastries provided by the company. Living Legends — especially those working office jobs — use their free time to *restore* health and fitness, not detract from it. Yet the Sunday brunch seems to collect the Legend-less, those huddling together during prime moments of freedom to down bacon bits and hash browns, sliding it all down with Tropicana orange "juice" (transferred from the original carton to a glass pitcher by the waiting staff so you think it's freshly-squeezed) and champagne (nothing to celebrate here — if anything, the scene warrants mourning).

My time in the Ivy League allowed me to see Sunday brunch for what it truly is. After months of sub-zero temperatures and overcast days, mid-April arrives in New England and the mercury finally strikes a bone-warming 55 degrees. The running paths along the Providence and Charles rivers are clear of snow and ice after the eight-month winter, and the collegiate athletic fields are ripe for a two-hour soccer game. Yet as the first long-awaited spring day finally takes hold, people are waking up feeling the worst they have ever felt. Their heads are throbbing. Their eyes are swollen. They're burping up the microwavable burritos they downed at 7-Eleven at 4am. Their knees are hurting from hours of standing and their feet are sorely swollen.

As the late morning light pierces the window, the New England student begins to open his dark, heavy eyelids, finally gaining enough strength to roll over.

He finds a stranger lying there, prompting him to think hard about the prior night in a frantic attempt to piece together the puzzle before the wretch gains consciousness. The only thing familiar is her mouth, which he can faintly recall moving tirelessly in a dimly-lit back corner of the Thirsty Turtle Underground — except now there's a lot more to contend with (and a lot more to dispose of) than a simple mouth.

The nude body — one all too familiar with the Ben and Jerry's Vermonster — begins to twitch. It moves more forcefully, turns its head, and sucks in a line of drool that was about to moisten the pillow. In the mind of the young New England student, there's only one method to resolve all that is wrong — the need to dispel this unsightly creature from his living quarters. He wills himself to forget about his bad feelings, lets go of his pride, and heads with his newfound companion to a local breakfast parlor (neutral territory where he can part with the beast hassle-free) for Sunday brunch.

From: Jon Brody
To: Jon Brody
Subject: NO PIZZA BOYS

It's 1:30am and you can't fall asleep because THERE ARE FOUR
SLICES OF PIZZA IN YOUR THROAT!!!
DO NOT DRIVE BY PIZZA BOYS AFTER LATE NIGHT WRITING
SESSIONS. You go to work in the library so (1) you can get away
from Ma and (2) you can focus on writing Legendary content. YOU
DON'T GO THERE TO BINGE EAT ON THE RIDE BACK HOME.
You are a public figure now. People are making note of every pound
you put on. Stick to your diet. If you eat something bad, cook it
yourself. I don't care what it is. Will always be better than eating
unhealthy food out somewhere.
You can't afford any more slip-ups.

From: Jon Brody
To: Trucker Sachs
Subject: Quick Question

Trucker,
I was working late on the book tonight and ended up at my local
pizza parlor. I never do this! I can't even remember the last time.
I feel so ashamed. Like such a hypocrite. How can I preach these
things if I'm not living them myself?
I know, I know, this may sound like a ridiculous question, and of
course we're coming at the world from opposite directions, but did
you ever find yourself just wanting to settle down, or stay in one
night — to not live the life you were advocating, be the person you
were trying to be on paper? How did you stay the course?

What happened when you had nights that you didn't trash yourself and have an unprotected hook-up? Did you doubt yourself? Did you feel like a fake? I'm trying to find that balance between being the guru that I'm aspiring to be, and being human at the same time.
Jon

From: Trucker Sachs
To: Jon Brody
Subject: RE: Quick Question

Jon,

It's an interesting dilemma, but not one you should stress over. Of course, as difficult as it was, there were some Mondays and Tuesdays that I didn't drink. But I knew I would make up for it later in the week. I knew on Thursday I would have twelve beers instead of ten, and on Saturday I would take nine shots instead of six. With your crazy fitness and diet routines, isn't there something extra you can do in future days to make up for the occasional slip-up?
Trucker

From: Jon Brody
To: Trucker Sachs
Subject: RE: RE: Quick Question

Trucker,

You're right: I will push harder this week. Just woke up and feel horrible. I'm so fat. Don't even think I can write a post today.
Jon

← PHOTO ↻

sportsfanatic4life

♥ 15 likes

sportsfanatic4life My happiness depends on the results of my home team...

> **lvnglgndry** Transition that happiness dependency to the results of your home scale.
>
> **sportsfanatic4life** Home scale? Wtf r u talking about?
>
> **lvnglgndry** Just flipped through your profile and you need to lose 40 pounds. Stop watching sports and start playing them.

The Living Legendary Framework, Manuscript Chapter 3: The Athletic Mindset

Day Camp

When Jon Brody graduated from the Ivy League, he had a difficult time figuring out the best way to continue playing sports. Brody had been an athlete his whole life and he didn't want to abandon the routines he had pursued for so many years. Yet it seemed like competitive, organized sports were only fostered in school environments, beginning in elementary school and ending in college. If you didn't have the skill set to become a professional athlete, you faced a dead end.

Jon Brody resolved to continue honing his athletic potential, professional options be damned. Under no circumstance would he become a weekend warrior or a gym rat — and so without any adult avenues available to him, Brody put his head down, bit his tongue, and joined an after-school program. The scene of a twenty-four-year-old running around the Astroturf with a group of middle-schoolers certainly seemed out of sorts, but Living Legends are never concerned with what other people think.

When the school year ended, Jon Brody was forced to go to summer camp. Living Legends aim to base themselves in rural or suburban areas, which always offer a plethora of athletic fields, tennis courts, and soft-surface running trails, and so it was no surprise to Brody when he discovered a camp being hosted in the city's outskirts. Living in his mother's apartment at the time in the downtown center (and refusing to drive due to the stiffening effects on the pedaling leg), Brody commuted via school bus with "tots" — the camp's youngest age group (8-10 years old).

The college-aged counselors — most five years Brody's junior — were perplexed as to why a grown man had enrolled in the camp — and further baffled by Brody's choice of transportation. At one point mid-summer, a concerned parent arranged alternative transportation when the school bus pulled up to the stop where she was waiting, her little boy fast asleep under the arm of a stubbled Brody, both of them resting their tired heads against the thumb-press windows in the last row after a particularly hot day.

It's not that Brody didn't try to make the best of his situation, because he did. Age aside, the Living Legendary founder had difficulty fitting in with his peers because of his strict nutritional regimen. See, at the end of each day, the ice cream truck would pull up beside the school buses fifteen minutes before departure. All of the campers (and primarily the tots from Brody's school bus), would flock there. Brody, isolated from the crowd during the popsicle selection and then empty-handed on the ride back, became an outcast. He looked on as his chocolate-faced companions laughed and bantered, seemingly having the time of their lives. But Brody didn't let this — or the fact that a caramel-covered drumstick wasn't part of his summer days — get to him, because the sacrifice was well worth it. He was on his way to Legendary.

or at least it's way harder

there's no way to be truly fit and work a 9-5. it's not just about the time — it's about the physical and mental destruction... physical in how stiff u get from sitting at a desk and the associated risk for injury, and mental in the daily grind of having to account to a boss/be in closed quarters for x number hours/deal with obese and unnecessarily stressed colleagues, etc.

Exactly. so how is that supposed to motivate me?

you need to figure out a way to make money not at a desk

If you take a trip to the Headquarters we can brainstorm...

Yea but you're not making any money from Living Legendary.

How are you financing all of this? That's what I want to know.

I'm investing in the product right now. But there will be a big payoff.

At that point I'm more than happy to finance you in a health-based venture

I do really want to take some time off and get back in shape. I guess I'll just have to do it in a few years...

You better do it now man. You're not getting any younger

Well thanks bud. That's super encouraging.

Someone's gotta be straight with you.

I'm investing in myself right now. With work and savings.

that's not self investment. That's a financial security blanket

I'd rather be financially secure than be a few pounds lighter!

My health is so important to me, but so are my career goals. The two don't reconcile perfectly

no they counter one another

In no way does pursuing a career benefit health — it destroys it

You know what Brody, I wish I could listen to you, I really do. But this is reality.

I don't have the time to hear your crap anymore

I'm just trying to help you.

You're living in a dreamland. I'm signing off.

What do you mean "signing off"?

3:00 PM

Look I take it back. I think what you're doing is right. I guess you just have to sacrifice your health for a bit longer

7:03 PM

Seriously man. Don't sign off

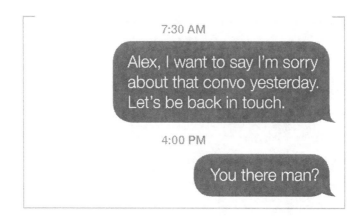

7:30 AM

Alex, I want to say I'm sorry about that convo yesterday. Let's be back in touch.

4:00 PM

You there man?

LivingLegendaryBlog.com

You Can Take My Life, But I'm Keeping the Watch

A well-educated child understands that his life carries more weight than material possessions, and he is taught to give away any valuables without hesitation were someone to hold him at gunpoint. Yet when it comes to the broader scope of life, people do just the opposite. Folks are trading away their health, and in turn their lives, for a bigger house or a more expensive car. They're determined to accumulate wealth at whatever cost — even if it's a heart attack at forty-five.

James is a friend from the Ivy League, and his father is one of the wealthiest bankers in the world. James's father groomed him to follow in his footsteps. He was granted admission to a prestigious college, internships at the nation's premier banks, and a full-time position upon graduation at the firm of his choice. By any conventional standard,

James was on his way to success. Yet if you held James's resume with him standing in front of you, your eyes wouldn't just see the paper. James is a walking icon of sickness: at 23, he's obese, deathly pale, covered in blemishes, and nearly immobile due to severe tendonitis in his knees. With all of his family's wealth and the vast resources at his disposal to hire lifestyle consultants, fitness experts, and dietitians, James hasn't seen a single one. He has fully abandoned his health for the benefit of his "career" — one that certainly won't be long-lived if he continues along his current trajectory.

There's a certain point at which the marginal value of each dollar gained declines… steeply. For James, it's not more money that will make a difference in his life, but rather the allocation of his time and energy into the right channels — namely to restore his ailing physical state. For James, hiring a troupe of health assistants would be pocket change, yet he hasn't sought out help. Why? Because his priorities are askew. James and his family don't even see the issue because all they can focus on are money, status, and prestige — things Living Legends care little for.

PHOTO

thehulkman

THAT MOMENT YOUR

PREWORKOUT KICKS IN

♥ 73 likes

thehulkman When my pre-workout kicks in

lvnglgndry @TheHulkMan if you need a
pre-workout drink you have no intrinsic willpower.
Living Legends can get through their workout
stimulation-free

---

thehulkman @LvngLgndry this is a joke right?

lvnglgndry No more of a joke than those artificial and processed ingredients you're guzzling every day in your protein shakes, fitness bars, and sports drinks

thehulkman @LvngLgndry Just looked at your photos. You're a scrawny piece of shit. I could crush your body with my bare hands. "Lean," as you call it, is weak. I'm squatting 400lbs daily and crushing it.

lvnglgndry @TheHulkMan With that knee brace I see? Your body is broken buddy.

thehulkman Better lock your doors Legend. Wasn't smart pinpointing the location on your last post

---

LivingLegendaryBlog.com

Find Anti-Role Models

Many would say I'm too critical of others. Sure, I'm critical — but my observations are made with an educational objective. I'm constantly looking to assist myself and other aspiring Legends reach full potential. Paying close attention to what's gone wrong in other people's lives can help you avoid falling victim to a similar scourge.

It's much more difficult in this day and age to find role models than it is to identify "anti-role models." "What's wrong with this picture?" is a lot more prevalent than "what's right?" All I internalize, I hardwire into my brain and use to construct my rules. Sometimes you have to see the negative to move towards the positive — and it's better to recognize the negative in someone else at the onset, than in yourself once it's too late.

COMMENTS (1)

CONTRADICTION

Hi Jon. I've been following the blog for quite some time now and I'm having difficulty understanding the relationship between pursuing a healthy, organic lifestyle and using Rogaine. Since you've become involved with the company, I've done some research on Rogaine and it doesn't seem to be a natural product. In fact, it appears as though it's quite toxic.

This just now came to mind because it seems as though what you advise in your blog posts is at odds with your advertisement contracts and — if you're a legitimate Rogaine user (which it seems you are) — your own lifestyle. If this isn't the definition of an "anti-role model," as you call it, I don't know what is.

From: Jon Brody
To: Jon Brody
Subject: Sleeping through your alarm?? GET IT TOGETHER!!

Sleeping through you alarm?? Are you stupid??? Legends don't sleep through alarms. You already wrote about that.
DO NOT DO THIS AGAIN. I don't care if you have to set five in a row. THERE IS NO MORE ROOM FOR ERRORS.

The Living Legendary Framework, Manuscript
Chapter 5: The Legendary Mental Approach

Compromised Mental Framework

Often times, aspiring Legends are plagued by a "Compromised Mental Framework" (CMF) — which ultimately curtails their impending progress and blocks them from reaching their full potential. Fortunately, tagging a CMF is relatively easy once you know what to look for.

Say you're looking forward to "National Chocolate Ice Cream Day," or you just sent somebody a "DTF" text. Maybe you find yourself driving a golf cart somewhere other than a golf course, or you've realized it's Saturday morning and you're inside a Hobby Lobby. Perhaps you're wearing a t-shirt you bought at an amusement park, or one that reads "Tattooed Dad," or "One Team. One Mission. Xbox 1." (and you don't work for Xbox). Or forget t-shirts because you're wearing a button down with short sleeves, or you just announced on national television, "American Ninja Warrior saved my life." If you "jumped when [you] shouldn't have" and incurred lasting physical damage, spend extensive time in "med spas," relate to the DJ Tiesto's lyrics, "I like us better when we're wasted," have "Beast Mode Lifestyle" spray painted to the hood of your car, find yourself waiting outside a Chipotle ten minutes before it opens, or are nonchalantly informing others of the season and year you "took a heart attack," or of "the time [you] stayed up for 36 hours straight" —

your mental framework is compromised.

I am always shocked by the breadth of CMFs that I encounter in my own inner circle. A good family friend — now in his early seventies — has become dangerously overweight over the past five years. When I ask him what he changed about his lifestyle, he responds, "well, now that I'm retired I feel like I deserve to eat whatever I want."

In another example, a good friend reasoned he should "never approach girls [he is] attracted to" because those girls won't go out with him — and so he limits his advances to only those women he's moderately attracted to — or even sometimes unattracted to — a mentality that has curtailed him from reaching his full romantic potential.

In yet another instance, a wealthy family I know that flies regularly on private charters tries to "get [their] money's worth" by filling up the seats with extended family members (who don't actually have any need — or even desire — to travel to the selected destination) and the cargo hold with expensive furniture pieces (even though there's no real need for the furniture to be transported — as it's simply being moved from one home to another, each of which is fully decorated). Worrying about filling up space on a private plane is a concern only the uber-wealthy could ever come up with.

Wealthy individuals misallocating resources on account of a CMF doesn't just apply to private charter flights — it's a problem more generally. Picture a high-powered businessman who buys his little girl a brand-new Range Rover for her eighteenth birthday. This won't facilitate Legend-building.

For the same money — likely less — he could have hired private tutors and physical trainers to help his daughter grow. Similarly, those who opt for luxury vacations fail to progress towards the Promised Land. Having a few weeks to oneself without the burden of work should not mean jetting off to a luxury hotel where your day will be spent eating, sleeping, laying around mindlessly by the pool, and drinking excessively.

One t-shirt from a vacation resort on the island of Tenerife (Spain) promoted the destination's well-known triathlon: "eat, drink [alcohol], and fuck." While I was in Tenerife for an athletic competition, I observed many of the English vacationers doing just that. What the shirt should have included as a fourth element was sunbathing to the point that you are thoroughly burnt to a crisp from head to toe, your corpulent body sufficiently pink so as to provide unquestioned resemblance to the mud-dwelling mammal so often accompanying the classic American breakfast.

From: Trucker Sachs
To: Jon Brody
Subject: Similar Titles List

Jon,

You're a dick. I spoke today with Danny Bezel, and he said you queried him with the book. When I told him I was helping you out, he shared your similar titles list. Calling me a "self-destructive personality" and "downright pathetic?" Are you fucking kidding?

I'm the one who's established here. I have the book. I have the following. You're nothing more than an ant. Trucker

LivingLegendaryBlog.com

Never Too Small To Store

To become a Living Legend, you must always be aware of your food portions and whether you really need those last few bites. It's always better to under-eat than over-eat, so pay close attention to the signs your body is giving you. There's a saying at the Living Legendary Headquarters: "It's never too small to store." So even if it's only one more bite but you're feeling full, put it in a container and save it for later.

A quick glance into the employee fridge at the Headquarters will reveal a collection of miniature glass Pyrex containers, each filled with small bites of food that didn't go wasted. A single walnut. The final two inches of a banana. Several strands of rice pasta. An avocado slice. The last bite of an oversized carrot.

COMMENTS (2)

WORTHLESS

I'm not sure what legend you're living here. Are you trying to promote YOUR lifestyle? This is overwhelmingly id-ridden ego spam. Another thing, before any readers take this guy's advice, I challenge you to challenge him to provide some credentials. My high school freshman nephew published a book (very few sold, but he did it!), that doesn't necessarily make you anyone with experience. Playing sports and working out is great! But we have thousands of elite athletes publishing stuff yearly, why listen to a guy who played sports in school when we can read things from dietitians, doctors, professional athletes, etc... If you want to be a sheep, follow on!

JON BRODY

I've held off for the most part responding to negative comments but this one, really, come on. Worthless — thanks for writing (and that's quite a name you have). Glad to know I've made it into the same category as your fourteen-year-old nephew, that's truly an honor. You're challenging everyone else to challenge me — but maybe you need to challenge yourself first and ask: What the hell am I doing logged on to LivingLegendaryBlog.com for an hour straight at five in the morning? If you're up at that hour and you're not working out, you would certainly benefit from some private consulting sessions — and I'd be happy to take you on free of charge as part of my philanthropic initiative.

You've managed to shed some interesting thoughts and I would urge you to participate in our dialogue going forward — whether it's over a midnight snack or in the midst of one of your early morning hazes. Sure, there are many Living Legends out there to learn from, and it's important to expand your knowledge base through all of the available materials. Hell, if you want a dietitian to usher you to the local Weight Watchers clinic or you want some medical practitioner to do a little lipo on you — that's a route you're always free to explore.

What I'm doing here is presenting logical methods for Living Legendary — methods that I have implemented in my own life to achieve my peak... in a healthy, enduring, and worthwhile manner. And I'm certain that my readership — you included, Worthless — can reach the same results. Also, I tracked your IP address and did a little investigation of my own — you're fat, bald, and broke. Congratulations on the trifecta.

LivingLegendaryBlog.com

The Power of Alone

You are the driver of your own path to Legendary, and nobody else can follow through with what's required but you. When it comes to working the body and the mind, you alone must invest the energy and time to produce the desired output. Sure, a knowledgeable mentor or a seasoned physical trainer can point you in the right direction, but at the end of the day you will be responsible for your own fate.

As the days pass with no book deal in sight, with those closest to me abandoning my side and my blog followers turning against me, it has become crystal clear that I must push through the dense terrain ahead alone. Yet my isolation, lack of support, and upstream current are no obstacle to my achieving what I've set out to. That's the power of Legendary. Sure, it would have been nice to have a book deal by now. Hell, I'm pretty confused why I don't. My message is powerful. My content is valuable. But I'm looking at the positive: the adversity will make me tougher in the end. Once you're at the top, you're alone anyway, so might as well spend your time getting there alone too.

It's a plain fact that Living Legendary means relying on yourself. Imagine Albert Einstein developing the Theory of Relativity inside a Starbucks while the patrons behind him argued about which type of coffee cake to split. Or Michelangelo painting the Sistine Chapel surrounded by a band of hooligans smoking weed and playing Xbox Live. Or Robert Frost writing "The Road Not Taken" while his friends threw back Fireballs and debated which nightclub to hit next.

In our modern era, it's even necessary to take it a step further by avoiding distractions like social media. If you're writing a memoir or you're researching a quantum mechanics paper, you must do so without a snapshot of Sally's morning Cronut on the Facebook newsfeed.

Those Transcendentalists were on to something: you don't need a stimulating environment to be stimulated. Many reason that growing intellectually and culturally is dependent upon the environment, and, because of this, flock to cities for the vast cultural offerings. What these people fail to realize is that how "cultured" or educated you are is a product of your own daily routines as an aspiring Legend, independent of your surroundings. If you're educated in how to educate yourself, a wooden cabin on Walden Pond is more than enough.

It's safe to say I'm in my own "cabin" at the Headquarters, yet in my case I'm actually trying to make contact with the outside world through my book. It's not just for my own sake, but for the aspiring Legends out there who don't have a voice to turn to. I'm their savior. Their leader. Their inspiration. Why can't these book agents see that? Why is nobody out there giving me a goddamn break?? It makes no sense.

It's probably just because I'm operating on a different wavelength. That's the only possible explanation. The people whose eyes I need to catch just can't relate. They're not Legendary. After all, how can you appreciate — or even understand — Legendary if you aren't a Legend yourself.

Living Legendary means realizing that if you understand the daily routines necessary for becoming a Living Legend and you can follow through with these routines without outside assistance, *there is no excuse for not being alone.* If you've spent the whole day toiling towards Legendary, take the evening off and socialize with friends. Talk to them about your struggle to become a Living Legend if you're so inclined. But under no circumstances should you try to convince yourself that you can become Legendary with some minion, sidekick, or BFFL plopped next to you, chomping away on a family size bag of Chex Mix. Living Legendary means focus, full investment, and undisturbed concentration. And it means never giving up.

TEN

LivingLegendaryBlog.com

Facebook as a Tool for Living Legendary

Spending time on Facebook is unproductive for aspiring Legends, certainly — yet the site can be used effectively as a tool to verify you are on the right path.

Profile-flip at random. Look through people's photos. Read their statuses. Glance at their "about" pages. Pay close attention to what information, and how much of it, is given. Then close your eyes and imagine yourself in their shoes. Complete this process for 20 random people. If you find yourself wishing you were in the shoes of *more than two*, you must adjust your lifestyle framework and start moving more aggressively in the direction of Legendary.

Share your own photos and statuses — and observe how many "likes" these posts generate. In short, the fewer likes you receive, the closer you are to Living Legendary. It's standard practice for people to "like" posts that are non-threatening, particularly ones that make them feel good *about themselves*. "Oh, look at Justin, that little chunkster. He's such a cutie!" Like. "Matt's going to the bar tonight and he's going to get shitfaced!" Like. "Sam is planning on watching football all day!" Like. At the end of the day, a "like" is nothing more than a person saying: "Oh, well that just made me feel comfortable. Now pass the potato chips."

Your goal as a Living Legend should be to surpass the Zero Like Threshold — the line after which your Facebook friends simply stop liking your posts. Once you've become a Living Legend you will know it because those you're connected with will no longer want to publicly commend your output. Or they will become "stumped" and lose perspective on how to respond at all.

If you just shared a photo of a bulging six-pack, don't expect many likes. If you just posted a status that you've "been elected President," or have "won the U.S. Open" — well, you probably won't be getting the appreciation you deserve.

From: Rick Sandell
To: Jon Brody
Subject: Living Legendary
Sent (Via Facebook Messenger):

Jon —
I'd like to preface this message by saying that I'm utilizing my time on Facebook for the sole objective of Living Legendary. That objective includes reaching out to you in order to explore your mind, a factory of Legendary Living, to see what I can extract. As you mentioned in one of your website videos, you were Living Legendary by making connections and that is what I hope to do in this note.

That being said, allow me to introduce myself. My name is Rick Sandell, I live in Forest Hills, New York, and I am a junior in high school, a highly competitive athlete and an all-star in the classroom.

I currently have a 4.6 GPA, I am the head of my own charity (Turkey Dinners to Take Down Hunger), and I am conversant in three languages (English, Spanish and Italian). I was introduced to you through Alex Miken — a former NYU athlete who competed against you once when you were in the Ivy League — when he directed me to your blog and videos with which I fell in love.

The demeanor and principles that you exhibit in each and every video and blog post are an inspiration to me to continue Living Legendary mentally and physically. After reading all of your posts and watching your videos, I started to spread the word about your genius to anyone who would take a minute to listen.

Back on subject, I aspire to attend the Ivy League. In fact, the hope of one day attending the Ivy League is the only thing that's keeping me alive these days — quite literally. I've been struggling a lot in recent years after my parents' divorce and my mom's breakdown. I don't come from a family of means, and after school I work two jobs so I can help put food on the table for my younger sister and brother. We currently live with my grandmother, but her social security checks only go so far. I feel alone in the world right now and I've been forced to take on incredible responsibilities for the sake of my family, and your blog has been pretty much my sole inspiration to keep going. There were many times when I thought about ending it all — I've been trying to figure out if it's possible to overdose on organic prune juice (I force my grandmother to buy organic juices, of course). So far I've been lucky, though, because I've come back to my senses and continued pushing. Legends never give up, like you say. They fight. I can assure you that I'm fighting every day thanks to your message.

You're my last hope. You're the only person in this world who I feel I can relate to and the only person who's message is worth embracing. I want to become a Legend and make it to the Ivy League. I want to rise above my modest beginnings, the unfortunate circumstances that I've been dealt, and become somebody. Not just for me, but for my family. I want to prove to my brother and sister that the world is a good place, where hard work, dedication, and discipline can get you somewhere.

I'm reaching out to you now because at this juncture I'm desperate for your mentorship and guidance and I have nowhere else to turn. As you attended the Ivy League and were an athlete there, I imagine you know the ropes of the recruiting process and how I can give myself the best chance of admission. I was wondering if you could gift me with some advice about what I can do starting TODAY to not only Live Legendary for personal health but to become enough of a Living Legend that the Ivy League would be eager to accept me. It would be greatly appreciated if I could pick your brain to see what I can be doing now and in the future to ensure the best chance of going to the Ivy League. Please help me. Out of the goodness of your heart, please help me get into the Ivy League. I would love to continue the tradition you began of Living Legendary in the Ivy League.

Best and thanks for your time,
Rick

From: Jon Brody
To: Rick Sandell
Subject: RE: Living Legendary
Sent (Via Facebook Messenger):

Hi Rick,

Thank you for the note and thanks for being a fan. You're worried too much about "the Ivy League."   Forget about the Ivy League and start investing in yourself. Never focus on results. Only effort. If you want more advice, you can read my book or it's $250/hour. Best of luck, Jon Brody

LivingLegendaryBlog.com

The Legendless Living Legend

A high school junior — Rick — recently wrote me a unique letter that sheds much insight into what it means to Live Legendary.

Rick's note was sent to me on Facebook — which he excused right away, explaining he only uses the site for Legend-building. No high school junior — I don't care how Legendary you are — is using Facebook *exclusively* in this manner. Even I — still a student of my own philosophies at Rick's age — spent plenty of time on the site photo-stalking girls and "poking" them (not Legendary courting practice, as you'll learn once the book is released).

Rick explained he wanted to "explore [my] mind" — something you should never say to a Living Legend. No Legend wants anyone inside his head. Rick said he wanted to "see what [he] could extract" from my brain, as if he were some tomb raider, plundering the treasures of a defenseless reserve. Sure, Ricky Boy had no doubt identified a bountiful source of wealth, but unfortunately that source didn't want anyone "exploring" or "extracting" from it.

Rick proceeded by revealing the laundry list of impediments that have curtailed him from reaching Legendary status. Rick's "been struggling a lot in recent years after [his] parents' divorce and [his] mom's breakdown." He "work[s] two jobs so [he] can help put food on the table for [his] younger sister and brother." Rick has also considered suicide: "There were many times when I thought about ending it all... So far I've been lucky, though, because I've come back to my senses and continued pushing."

Come on, now. I don't care about your family problems, about your mother or brother or sister, there are simply no excuses when it comes to reaching the Promised Land. Either you can or you can't. There's no in between. They're called "Living Legends" for a reason.

I can say with certainty that Rick was a long way away from where he needed to be, even though he significantly inflated his credentials in his note. "Competitive" alone didn't seem to suffice in describing his abilities on the athletic field. He needed "highly" to boot. A quick background check revealed Rick actually sucked at sports. Rick started his own charity, too. Or so he said. Nothing appeared in Google to match the description.

What was most disturbing about Rick's note was his incessant referencing of the Ivy League and his desire to attend. All Rick could think about, write about, or discuss was "the Ivy League." In all his efforts to inflate his credentials and exaggerate his difficulties, Rick had lost touch with the most crucial component of Living Legendary: investing in the process. Rick wasn't finding passion, he wasn't pursuing self-growth, and he wasn't focusing on becoming a true Living Legend. Rick was just thinking about where his efforts would bring him, and he had become consumed by the end result.

You have to remember that investing in Living Legendary *doesn't guarantee anything* with respect to results. You need to focus on Living Legendary because you want to Live Legendary. Doing so should be independent of any and all outcomes you hope to achieve.

Rick didn't write to me to "[make] connections," as he explained in the note. He certainly wasn't hoping to sit down with me to a cup of tea on Walden Pond. Rick was contacting me with a clear-minded agenda. He wanted to enter my head, cherry pick what appealed, and then throw my carcass to the wolves while he plotted and planned exactly how he was going to catapult himself out of his cognition-less, parent-less misery in some Forest Hills retirement ghetto (did I mention he's living with grandma?). At the end of the day, Rick didn't give a shit about me or a shit about Living Legendary. All he cared about was building a heavily exaggerated, Legendless resume to deceive Ivy League admissions officers.

One great bonus that comes along with Legendary is having the intuition to separate your ilk from the imposters. The true aspirants from the parasites that want to suck you dry.

I hate to break it you to Ricky Boy, but you ain't getting in.

COMMENTS (4)

CHRIS

IS THIS REAL? Jon Brody you're a fucking asshole.

MEREDITH

At first when I was reading this I thought it was a joke. Then I realized it wasn't. A young, desperate high-schooler writes you for advice and you throw him under the bus like this? You're Satan.

DICK

Eat a dick Brody.

TOM ALLINGTON

How dare you bash the hopes and dreams of this young man! When you had few credentials as a high school athlete and you played in my showcase, nobody put you down. Nobody told you that you wouldn't make it. Now you went to the Ivy League and you think you're so great that you can destroy someone's aspirations like this? And on top of it do this to poor Rick, who's been dealt a such a hard hand in life?? How dare you. I'm embarrassed to say that you're an alumnus of my event.

From: Trucker Sachs
To: Jon Brody
Subject: We're Finished

Jon,

I just saw the Legendless Living Legend post. What the FUCK do you think you're doing? What if I did that to you, posting an embarrassing bit on my site about how you're an incompetent little shit who's never going to get a book published! And used your name! I'm pretty sure you wouldn't feel so good. We're done here. I'm not going to give back to someone who doesn't want to give back himself. Plus you're a fucking asshole. That guy is really struggling, man.

Take care of yourself. Trucker

Cardboardmag.com/Brody_Slams_Young_Fan

Earlier this week, Jon Brody wrote a post in which he tore down a suicidal seventeen-year-old high school student — Rick — who sent him an e-mail reaching out for advice with his college applications to the Ivy League. The Living Legendary founder excerpted Rick's note in his blog, revealing that the young man is helping to financially support two younger siblings in the wake of his parents' divorce. In spite of it all, Brody proceeded to bash Rick publicly in front of millions, labeling him a "Legendless Living Legend" and stating he had no chance at Ivy League admission. The post has provoked much outrage, as many believe the attack was unwarranted and cruel. Nevertheless, the post has drawn huge publicity (albeit all of it negative) towards the blog. Our radar is now pointed towards the Headquarters to see what stunt Jon Brody will pull next.

LivingLegendaryBlog.com

Arouse Emotion

One simple question can help you gauge whether or not you're Living Legendary: am I arousing emotion in those around me? The emotion itself is irrelevant — joy, hate, love, excitement, rage, awe, resentment, jealously, curiosity — so long as you are affecting others significantly enough to elicit an emotional response.

Unfortunately, those who enjoy great success — and ultimately become Living Legends — often have haters. When we see our neighbor acquire riches, we become jealous and want them too, a normal human response. But keep in mind that "riches" don't just pertain to material wealth, but also intangibles like status, admiration, respect, and power. Living Legends are always on the receiving end of emotion — and under no circumstances do they waste time and energy emotionally responding to others. As an aspiring Legend, you should strive to have those in your inner circle investing emotion into you, what you're doing, and what you're accomplishing. If you find they are, you are well on your way.

Over the last year, many haters have surfaced on the Living Legendary blog, indicating that the site has been a huge success. Each week, more and more livid personalities surface — and the numbers are astounding. The haters — always anonymous under a pseudonym — are seething, on-edge, emotionally-consumed individuals harboring deep-seated resentment — and they have begun to channel their frustration directly onto the LivingLegendaryBlog.com discussion boards. I couldn't have asked for a better outcome.

COMMENTS (2)

BRIAN JOHNSON

"Under no circumstances do [Living Legends] waste time and energy emotionally responding to others." Yet you participate in name calling arguments all the time.

BLACK KETTLE

Have to agree with Brian here. Pot calling the kettle black?

From: Roy Brody
To: Jon Brody
Subject: A Note From Your Family

Hi Jon,

This message is being sent from Uncle Brody's email account on behalf of the entire Brody family — your loving Aunt and Uncle and Cousins. We have all talked about the contents of this email at length, and we all genuinely hope that you will spend time reading and thinking about our message, as it is the sum of considerable discussions between all of us. Over the span of your whole life, we have enjoyed great times with the family in all different places, which produced some fabulous memories. Whether it was at the beach in California, or quality moments in Cincinatti, Atlanta, or Charlotte, we have all done only one thing: love you. There has never once been an instance when we have ever expressed anything but tremendous support and love for you and all of your pursuits. Whether it was playing a boardgame, going to the ice-cream parlor, watching a movie, attending a football game, or just enjoying a fun time around the living room TV with a "Friends" marathon, we have all fostered a truly special and intimate familial bond.

None of us can remember a single time when there was a malicious remark, or anything short of complete support for one another at any time in our lives. Across all of the years, we have all had a direct and trusting relationship, which naturally involved speaking freely and openly. Lisa and Jessica have always shared their innermost feelings and life problems with you to foster a strong familial bond. Your Uncle and Aunt have talked freely with you about life, as well as the many obstacles it presents. Even Uncle Harry and Cousin Harry, before they passed, always took the time to share with you a kind word or piece of advice (understandably, we know you never listened to Uncle Harry's diet recommendations).

A few months ago, you eagerly called us up to tell us about your book project. You said "we would love what you had written and that we would come away learning many life lessons..." Back when we spoke, we were all truly happy for you and, as always, were behind you 100% in whatever path you chose to follow. We were also curious as to when we would be able to read it and you responded, "I will be sending everyone a signed copy once it is released." Some time after this discussion, passages from the book were read that centered on stories of what is obviously an account of Lisa and Jessica.

We were shocked by what we read and could not understand how you could have the nerve to present them so negatively in the book. We are all very much worried that you don't fully understand the repercussions of your unfavorable portrait of us and what an extended effect it could have on us emotionally, socially, and professionally. And so we say to you, what have we done to you to deserve such a thing? To start with, the factual accounts are incorrect. Second, you must remember that we are private citizens and not you or anybody else has the right to reveal any medical history, consultations, treatments, or health issues of any kind to anyone. The idea that your book would contain hurtful and revealing information about any of us is a huge betrayal of trust, especially between loving family members who have never done anything malicious to you to warrant such actions on your part.

To look down the barrel at Lisa over the struggles with her body hair, commenting that she looks like a "distant human ancestor," is not how she or anyone else would want to be described. To present the story of a struggling Jessica who has difficulty making it through a day is wrong and hurtful, especially to someone who has the kindest heart in the world. You have presented a picture of her that is factually incorrect and does not represent the respected professional and cared for woman that she is.

If this book is released for general consumer use, she could become victim to grave consequences from your erroneous presentation of her life and efforts to reveal medical information that you don't have any right sharing. Both Lisa and Jessica have read the passages about them and they are shocked. They can't understand why you would use them as pawns to promulgate your own philosophies. We are all truly proud of what we have achieved in our lives, enjoy many friendships with people who respect us, are influential members in our communities yet you aim to inaccurately paint us all in a very hurtful and slanderous manner. None of us can believe you would have the nerve to do something like this.

While you may respond by thinking that our letter is unwarranted, it means very much to us. You have betrayed our trust, and we do not want any depictions of us released in a public forum... not in your blog, book or any other public outlet you may choose to pursue in the future. All of us are private citizens who have the right to keep our privacy. We are still your caring family but need you to assure us that nothing you write or release will contain descriptions that in any way reflect any of us. Thank you for doing the right thing. We hope you enjoy success as a best selling writer, but without any material anywhere about the four of us.

From: Jon Brody
To: Michael Brody
Subject: Book

You shared your copy with Uncle Roy, Aunt Hillary, and the cousins?? I printed that out for YOUR EYES ONLY. You had ZERO right doing this. The book was NOT ready for anyone else to see.

LivingLegendaryBlog.com

Father Brody

Father Brody is a homosexual with a long gray beard who divorced his wife (Ma Brody) of twenty years when he decided to come out of the closet. He wears a *yarmulke* at all times, attends synagogue Wednesday through Saturday, and eats a pastrami sandwich on rye at the kosher deli every day for lunch (no surprise, he's obese). Father Brody wasn't always a religious zealot with *tzitzit* hanging from his belt, though. His devotion to God came on suddenly — precisely one year after he blackmailed a former romantic partner — then the CEO of Citibank with a wife and kids — by threatening to make their relationship public and ruin his repuation. Father Brody received a $15 million wire transfer to keep his mouth shut, and more likely than not, he felt a bit guilty.

Father Brody "works" out of a small office in a not-for-profit Jewish organization's upper east side brownstone. He managed to convince several board members to lend him office space on the promise that he would help raise money for the foundation, yet so far he hasn't brought in a dime. Father Brody could certainly make a donation himself if he wanted — after all, he is a wealthy man. But he's hoarding his settlement money and living off the interest so he doesn't have to find a real job. Eating into the principle for the purposes of philanthropy wouldn't make much sense.

Over the last decade and a half, Father Brody has pursued a

series of dead-end ventures — ranging from quirky invention ideas to business propositions he pitched to companies — none of which ever materialized. To his family and friends, Father concealed the fact that his wealth didn't come from a legitimate source. Nobody asked any questions, and Father outwardly maintained the image of a successful entrepreneur.

Father Brody's Legendless physical, personal, and professional path, combined with his false portrait of himself to the world, has been instrumental in shaping the Living Legendary founder's world view — and ultimately, the Framework. Jon Brody has placed Father front and center in his mind as an example of what not to become — and having such a story within his family history has served to fuel his own Legendary pursuits, as well as his encouragement of others'.

From: Michael Brody
To: Jon Brody
Subject: PICK UP!!

Jon — you're not taking my calls… Cousin Jessica just sent me the blog post. TAKE IT DOWN NOW!! This will have longer lasting implications if you don't act immediately….
Sent from my iPhone

The Living Legendary Framework, Manuscript
Chapter 9: Legendary Romance

Avoid "Love"

Living Legends pursue their romantic lives with care and caution. Legends understand that the concept of "love" is just a marketing ploy to sell more product (Valentine's day roses, anniversary dinners, engagement rings, surprise chocolates, etc.) and in turn separate sex from some grander scheme. The expression, "making love," was coined to make this primitive act sound civilized, but for Living Legends, sex is nothing more than the physical act. While this may seem callous, Legends maintain this philosophy because they understand where this "path of love" leads. For the man, it's fatherhood — a concept that itself is both unnatural and psychologically destructive. On your next trip to the park, look deep into the eyes of the mute man tagging along five meters behind his wife and eldest child, pushing a stroller with the newborn. When you head to the supermarket this evening, make note of the parking lot soldier, humbly repositioning the child seat with one arm while loading the twenty-five grocery bags with the other, his female lieutenant looking on intently to secure the job complies with procedural specification. Both scenes are brief windows into the psychology of a crushed spirit — one void of optimism, vigor, and hope for future enjoyment. At the end of the day, the "Family Man" is nothing more than a conquered individual who — stripped of all that he had once loved and enjoyed — mistakenly comes to believe (or at least convinces himself) that procreating and tending to his offspring is his purpose (and not only that, but one that gives him "joy").

Legendary is — and always has been — the pursuit of something unique. There's nothing unique about reproducing. Sure, some will argue that bearing a child is the quintessential act of uniqueness given that each new baby is unique himself. But it's important to remember that 99.9% of these children — no matter how unique upon exiting the womb — are headed to the same destination: a quarter-century old, obese, unproductive, bald, pre-diabetic running on five or six prescription medications (which almost always includes an anti-depressant).

Cardboardmag.com/Brody_Father_Responds

At the end of last week, Jon Brody turned up the heat again on the Living Legendary Blog by undercutting his own father, labeling him "Legendless" and revealing him to be a blackmailer and fraud. The article comes just a few short weeks after a controversial incident in which Brody verbally assaulted a young follower who reached out to him for support. The pair of posts have generated much backlash on the Living Legendary discussion boards, and many are now boycotting the site because of them. The Cardboard Mag investigative unit blindsided Jon Brody's father — Michael Brody — coming out of

Shabbat services early yesterday morning, and he reluctantly gave two minutes of his time between bites of free chocolate rugelach (he had somehow amassed six in each hand) that the family of that week's bar mitzvah had provided to congregation members post-service.

CM: Mr. Brody, how has all of this affected you?

MB: I am a private citizen, and this has been an embarrassment. I am very disappointed in Jon. He has acted without forethought and has failed to fully analyze the implications of his actions.

CM: The facts that pertain to you in his post, are they true?

MB: They are private. That is what matters. Jon is a hypocrite. Years after graduating from college, he still lives with his mother, and off her money. He hasn't earned a cent. His book isn't published and his blog hasn't generated any income at all. He is, as the younger generation might say, a loser.

CM: While the blog hasn't generated income, it is certainly successful — recently passing the four million monthly views marker. Are you at all proud of what your son has accomplished, family controversy aside?

MB: Accomplished? Getting people to read free garbage on the Internet isn't an accomplishment in my book. Jon isn't providing any value to the world — he's just hurting himself and his family.

CM: Is there anything else you would like to say to Jon Brody or his audience?

MB: Please read through Jon's material with a cautious eye. He is very young, immature, and inexperienced — and he has an agenda. He always has. I love him, but I don't like the person he's become. An Ivy League degree didn't make him any better than his father. I even have a Wikipedia page.

From: Margaret Sandstrom
To: Jon Brody
Subject: RE: Query

Dear Jon,

It's been a long time and nice to hear from you! I will tell Sam you wrote me — will you be going to the five-year reunion next month? Thank you for contacting me as a "last resort" and I did glance through the material you sent. Unfortunately I am not connecting with it. To say love isn't real and that people shouldn't aspire to become parents is quite off-putting — and certainly not a message any trade publisher will endorse. Plus, it's unlikely that the typical college kid will be interested in hearing long-winded stories about your cousins and uncles. I agree with what other agents have told you about your credentials — it's a bit premature for you as a non-fiction writer. Please send my regards to your parents.

Wishing you all the best,

Margaret

From: Jon Brody
To: Richard Thurston
Subject: Hi Professor Thurston

Hi Professor Thurston,

As a senior two years ago, I was a student in your American Drama Since '45 class and received an A. (I'm sure you remember me — I was the one you asked to stop "carrot munching" during lecture.) Since graduating, I've written a book that I've been aiming to get published, and it feels as though the light at the end of this tunnel is non-existent, no matter how hard I push. I've sent query letters to hundreds of agents and editors, most of whom haven't responded, and those who have do not wish to take on my work. I know you have extensive connections in the publishing industry, and figured I would reach out on the off chance you could help.   Whatever you can do would be greatly appreciated. Also, I want to let you know that in looking back at all the classes I took during my time in the Ivy League, yours was certainly the most memorable.

Thank you.

Jon Brody

LivingLegendaryBlog.com

Overcoming Erotica

Because of their strong mental resolve and self-belief, Living Legends are never distracted by obstacles. It's how you deal with adversity that will determine whether or not you reach the top.

Over the last year, in addition to my blog posts, I've worked to send out query letters to hundreds of agents for my book. Not a single one has agreed to represent me. There is a crisis in Legend-building today, as the majority of our talented youth are falling short in their endeavors because they don't have a relatable, inspiring voice to guide them. Clearly, these literary agents are afflicted by the same illness.

Instead, they publish heaps and heaps of erotica. I believe it must be the case that the publishing industry — fragile due to the rise of the Internet — is financed by group of overweight, embittered, sex-starved women desperate for soft-core porn. They don't want to watch real porn because seeing young, attractive, sexually-responsive twenty-year-olds enjoying amazing sex would make them feel bad about their lives. Instead, they want to read about it in a novel, where the characters aren't real and the sexual scenes pretend to be in the service of a "plot."

The erotica-dominated book industry, coupled with its anorgasmic female gatekeepers, has become a major hurdle in Jon Brody's quest to expose the Living Legendary Framework to the world. Yet he will keep pushing. No obstacle, no matter how great, will curtail him of reaching his final destination.

Why you're sticking with it:

- Never forget why you started: to become the first "author rock star." Selling out stadiums for book readings.

- The goal: to "make reading cool again."

- Your break will eventually come. All u need is Kanye to give a single mention he's "Living Legendary," and then you're home free.

- Stick to the dream: you on the cover of every magazine in America with your shirt off and six-pack abs bulging, pointing at the camera: "Jon Brody. Living Legendary."

- A fake-tit signing booth at book readings.

- Naked, lean-armed girls waiting in line to feed you organic strawberries after a three hour workout.

- Throwing out signed organic bananas into the crowd.

- Telling late-night tv hosts they're obese when they probe if you have a real job.

The Living Legendary Framework, Manuscript Dedication Page

This book is dedicated to the aspiring Living Legend. Keep toiling.
Don't lose faith.

From: Paulson Hauckbauer & Rose
To: Jon Brody
Subject: Legal Notification

Mr. Brody,

This letter is being sent on behalf of Michael Brody and the Brody
family to notify Mr. Jon Brody that a case has been filed against
him in New York State District Court 32 on three separate counts of
defamation, invasion of privacy, and breaching of medical records in
the form of literary materials, and one count of slander and unlawful
revelation of details pertaining to a past settlement in the form of digital
media/online article. You will hear more from us and the court once a
pre-trial conference has been arranged. Regards, Huck Hauckbauer

From: Smiling Feet
To: Jon Brody
Subject: No More Smile

Hi John. this smiling feet. We get you email in Legend site. We let you
know you no more welcome in smiling feet. One other client work
book agency. he say you write very bad story talking bout smiling feet.
Owner say he no want you back no more.

Smiling feet

Thoughts:

- You're feeling burned out. But you need to keep pushing. You're close.

- Problem is isolation. Nobody to talk to anymore. Ma wants you out. Maxi gone. Trucker out. Alex not responding. Brody's suing. No Smiling Feet.

- Think hard about Dr. Trap's comments a few years back at Ivy League psych services. Read up on "exercise addiction." She might have been on to something. (But don't forget she was obese. Maybe she just couldn't relate.)

- Regardless, you can't take many more days of this. You're living in solitary confinement. Very clear now why they use this for torture.

- Put writing on hold for a few days. Start brainstorming how to resolve this.

TWEETS	FOLLOWING	FOLLOWERS	FAVORITES	LISTS
452	5K	81K	1,035	4

Tweets   Tweets & replies   Photos & videos

Living Legendary @LvngLgndry · 1h
@KanyeWest **Kanye: It's time to start Living Legendary. How about a retweet?** #livinglegendary #retweet #desperate

↩ 0   ♺ 0   ★ 2

From: George Janglevoss
To: Jon Brody
Subject: Assault

Mr. Brody,

With assault charges now pending from your actions in the mediation room, our failure to reach a resolution is now the least of our problems. As I mentioned to you the other day, our course of action will depend upon how much of the damage to your father's face is permanent, and we will only know this once the bandages are removed.

Writing now as your friend, not your lawyer: What the hell were you thinking? I'll admit it was quite the blow, "Legendary" I suppose you might say — but that hot-headed explosion has now killed us in terms of having any chance to win this case. Unless you're willing to settle, I won't be able to represent you.

Best regards,

George Janglevoss

From: Jon Brody
To: Samuel Gross
Subject: Exclusive Privileges

Hi Mr. Gross,

If you're interested in looking at the manuscript on an exclusive basis you can. I hope to hear from you. Jon Brody

From: Jon Brody
To: Anthony Griegos
Subject: Restaurant Mentor

Dear Mr. Griegos,

I found your name on the Ivy League alumni network and I'm contacting you because I saw you have a restaurant in the Miami area. After graduating two years ago, I wrote a book that I tried publishing — but it didn't end up panning out in the way I thought. I am now looking for a more practical route and given my interest in health and nutrition I thought the restaurant business might be a good one to pursue. I've been brainstorming and came up with an idea for a dessert parlor that sells frozen organic whole fruit — banana, pear, apple, mango, grapes — in an effort to give people a healthy alternate to ice cream and sorbet. What do you think of the name "Legendary Licks?" If you had time, I was hoping you might serve as a mentor to me in this process.

 I look forward to meeting you and thanks for your time.

Regards,

Jon Brody

Cardboardmag.com/HulkMan_Takes_Down_Brody

It has been reported that Jon Brody is in the hospital today after a physical confrontation with one of his Instagram followers — TheHulkMan. According to eyewitnesses at the scene (a South Miami sidewalk), TheHulkman, twice Brody's size and weight, lifted the Living Legendary Founder over his head, proceeding to throw him down onto the hood of a car — much like a move you might see at a World Wrestling Federation match.

From inside sources we know that Brody and TheHulkMan were involved in a heated exchange on the social networking site, which prompted TheHulkMan — a Venice Beach-based weightlifter who's made a name for himself in the nutritional supplement industry as a whey protein promoter — to fly across the country so he could meet Jon Brody face-to-face at his doorstep.

With the heat that Brody's been taking in recent months, it seems as though an incident of this nature has been a long time in the making.

LivingLegendaryBlog.com

Public Apology

I am writing to apologize publicly to my readership on LivingLegendaryBlog.com. Over the past year on my blog (and the past two with my book), my primary objective has been to better the lives of others. I have sought to provide those in the dark with a feasible path towards reclaiming health, finding passion, and maximizing potential. For whatever reason, my ideas and methods haven't been embraced. In many ways, the opposite has occurred — a great number of people have become offended, angry, and hurt by my words. I myself have dealt and suffered real, physical hurt from the things I've said.

Last night at the hospital (I'm sure you all have seen the news by now), I stayed up late and re-read my posts over the last year, along with all of the comments. After internalizing it all, I want to say that I sympathize with those on my discussion boards and I am truly, truly sorry.

At the end of the day, Living Legendary was really just about trying to stay alive myself. The world is sick. I grew up being told that with enough doctors' visits, psychiatrist sessions, private tutors, restaurant meals, medications, internships, quack physical trainers, and pep talks from vacant family members, I could have it all: the Ivy League, a corner office, and a Range Rover. But who decided that was what "having it all" should mean?

The world is sick. The mainstream media and advertising industry brainwash people into throwing away their time and money on empty promises and self-destructive behavior. Capitalism is sick. My motivation to write a book and pursue this blog wasn't completely altruistic, I must admit. It wasn't altruistic at all. It was a way for me to find a way out, make a living on my own time and on my own terms to preserve my well being. People are engaged from a young age in a rat race with no end in sight. They have no time because they have a two-hour commute and ten more (if they're lucky) at the desk. They have no energy because they're forced to sit all day, on someone else's schedule, for someone else's profits. And they have no optimism — which is why when the weekend finally arrives, their first impulse is to reach for a drink.

With my writing, I figured I could stay around my home (or my mother's, at least) to prepare my own healthy food, I could have a significant enough chunk of time in the morning to do a proper workout, I could have a purpose other than going out on Fridays and Saturdays, and I could stay healthy. If I could succeed as a writer, I could guarantee my own health — while at the same time, maybe, if anyone else was as crazy as me, contribute something truly positive and useful to the world.

Unfortunately, sometimes, no matter how hard you try, you can't make that difference if the circumstances don't allow you to. I suppose it boils down to that clichéd expression, "A fish doesn't know it's wet." The people I needed to get my message out, the gatekeepers to reaching an audience, and igniting a Living Legendary movement were the same people consumed by the structure that I sought to bring down. They couldn't see the value in my words because all they wanted was a sure bet — another M.D. telling people that being fat is okay, or an Oprah-sponsored dietitian advising the masses that the path to weight loss is her brand-new, patented diet bar.

To be Legendary, you have to have control. Of your food. Your time. Your surroundings. And ultimately, your life. That's what this society has become expert in taking away: your control. And that's what I wanted to preserve for myself. Control. Over my life... and, I suppose, over yours. That's where I went wrong. I can't force the world to change if it doesn't want to. I can't make you see the light if you're happy to be stuck in the dark. I can't help you if you'd rather resist than let me in. I CAN'T KEEP CLICKING ON MY BLOG TO INCREASE THE NUMBER OF VISITS BECAUSE I NEED TIME TO STEAM MORE VEGETABLES.

Sorry. I guess even in my apologies I can get carried away. I would like all of my fans and enemies on the Living Legendary blog to know that I will be shifting my life's focus in a new direction. I'm not abandoning the blog and I'm not abandoning you. I've just recognized it's time to move on. Maybe I can take up a new sport. Fencing, perhaps.

I'm not quite sure what my next step will be, but I will work hard to make sure my future efforts make a difference in the world. I will continue striving for Legendary, as should you. I want to wish you all the best of luck.

Keep Living Legendary. And stop being fat.

Yours truly, Jon Brody

COMMENTS (1)

CASSANDRA

Since the start of the blog, I've popped in weekly to see your intriguing content. I consider myself to be a casual shopper at this point where I pick and choose certain things you mention and try to implement them into my life because maybe all of it would be too drastic a change for me. That maybe small steps can help me to achieve a better lifestyle. I realize the 100% effort mentality and how my succumbing to old weaknesses and habits is unraveling my current efforts, but I believe that as I adopt certain things over the weeks/months/years, I will be there, or closer to there. Thank you for being a source of guidance. I know some of it I don't agree with and find hard to swallow, but that leads me to the next point.

What I most wanted to mention was the medium and communication. In real life I'm a bubbly personality. When I add a facial expression, tone of voice, and hand gestures in real life, people can see and hear the way I'm telling a story. On a written forum, those things are lost and words are it. You can't necessarily take the author's work and see how they would communicate it to you in person, so sometimes on paper you come across as really extreme, but in reality for all I know you might be a very normal and fun conversation in real life. Anyhow, I appreciate the post and your commitment to helping others. At the end of the day, you're doing work to better the lives of yourself and everyone who follows, how little or much they do, and that's more than most people can say.

From: Jon Brody
To: Maxi
Subject: Love

Dear Maxi,

I'm writing this over email because I knew I couldn't express what I needed to in a text. I've been thinking a lot about you since we've been apart, and I want to get back together if you think it could work. I have strong feelings for you. I would even go so far as to say I "love" you. I want to move forward together and see where these feelings take us.

You don't need to do my fitness program anymore. You don't even have to work out at all if you don't want to. When it comes to Living Legendary, I've realized that I can only account for myself. There's just no way to make other people Legendary. I also want you to know that there won't be any more pressure to do quirky sexual stuff. We can stay traditional :-) .

I hope you consider us again and we can have a reunion date. I'll be back from the hospital tonight and plan on filling up the fridge with organics, so we can have a hearty meal at the Headquarters ;-).

Much Love. Jon

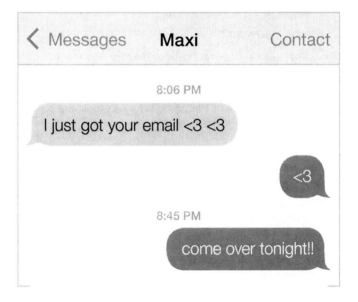

From: Trucker Sachs
To: Jon Brody
Subject: Book Deal

Hey, man, long time. Some crazy publisher offered me my own imprint
and I need some controversial shit to put out there. Not sure what your
status is, but if you're still interested….book deal?

About the Author

Jon Pearlman is a former #1 singles player for the Harvard tennis team and ATP-ranked touring professional. Jon is the founder of Creating Substance, a fitness and nutrition brand. He lives in South Florida. *Living Legendary* is his debut novel.

CPSIA information can be obtained
at www.ICGtesting.com
Printed in the USA
FFOW01n2324230417
34782FF